I0580157

THE FAERIE RACE BOOK TWO

THE ELEMENTAL TRIAL

CLAIRE LUANA
J.A. ARMITAGE

The Elemental Trial

Copyright © 2019 by Claire Luana and J.A. Armitage

ISBN: 978-1-948947-73-2 (Paperback)

ISBN: 978-1-948947-72-5 (Ebook)

All rights reserved. Except as permitted under the U.S. Copyright Act of 1976, no part of this publication may be reproduced, distributed or transmitted in any form or by any means, or stored in a database or retrieval system without the prior written permission of the author.

All characters appearing in this work are fictitious. Any resemblance to real persons, living or dead, is purely coincidental.

Cover Design: Covers by Juan

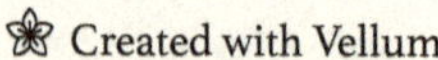 Created with Vellum

1

———

I sat on the floor, holding a potted fern, talking to a magic bunny. No, the Fantastic Faerie Race hadn't driven me completely insane. Though, there were still two more trials that could claim that distinguished honor.

I closed my eyes again, blowing out a long breath. I had no idea what time it was; my room in Hennington House didn't have a clock, and my phone was across the room. I thought it was morning. In my mind's eye, I saw the etheric rabbit that represented my magic—my power over the element of earth. In the past few hours of my pathetic efforts, the rabbit had grown much more comfortable with me, which seemed weird because it was all in my head. Wasn't it?

The plant was nestled between my crossed legs. I was trying to move the dirt inside the pot using my magic. I needed the bunny's help for that, which thus far, had not been forthcoming. Orin had told me that when he was a kid, he'd used magic by imagining the different elements as pets. It had worked for me in the dragon's lair on Emerald Mountain at the end of the last trial. I needed to be able to recreate it at will. Hence, plant. Hence, bunny. "Come on," I coaxed. "Look at this wonderful dirt! So fragrant and full of nutrients. Don't you want to move it? Let's move it together."

I knew I should be sleeping, but I'd given up on that after about three hours of tossing and turning. My mind, assaulted by flashbacks of my days over the Hedge, refused to shut down to allow me to get some much-needed rest. And I did need it. I wouldn't have the luxury of a warm comforter or a soft mattress for long. The FFR had allowed us two nights back in Wales to recuperate before we were to be thrown back into Faerwild and into the second trial of the race.

It wasn't as though I wasn't tired—on the contrary, I was completely exhausted. But every time I closed my eyes, I saw Zee's unblinking stare gazing up to the sky, or a swarm of piranha-like Red Caps trying to eat Duncan and Yael alive. Being trapped in an endless magic cave with no end in sight. Being chased by a panther. Being chased by an ancient tree-like faerie king. Being chased—and caught—by a dragon. And then, there was Cass's letter. If I was going to be honest with myself, it wasn't the danger of the next trial that had my mind whirring—it was the letter that Cass had written to Genevieve, and folded into the shape of a flower just the way she used to send messages to me when we were little. A pang of jealousy cut me as I thought of the note again. It meant she was alive—which was the part I was concentrating on...but that knowledge brought another question. Why hadn't she tried to contact me? Two years had passed without a word.

The bunny started to hop away as my mind wandered. "Wait!" I said to it, gesturing it back. "I'm sorry. You're such a pretty bunny." It turned and hopped back towards me in my mind, its little nose quivering. It *was* adorable. It sniffed my proffered hand, and then—to my shock, it hopped into my arms. I let out a gasp of delight, stroking its soft fur. "Should we move some dirt?" I swear its little nose quivered in affirmation. I focused on the plant, pulling the power through the rabbit in my mind, and channeling it into the dirt. I just wanted to raise it into the air slightly. I cracked one eye to peek and gasped as I saw that the dirt around the fern's base was, in fact, floating ever so slightly.

A knock sounded on the door, and I yelped in surprise. The bunny leapt from my mental arms and dirt flew everywhere. I closed my eyes as it rained down on me. I sighed.

The knock sounded again. "Just a minute," I called. I opened my eyes, brushing dirt off my face and lashes. I had exploded the potted fern. "Great," I grumbled, standing and shaking off the dirt and bits of plant as best I could.

I swung open the door and, to my surprise, found Ben standing there. I hadn't seen him since we left Faerwild. All the camera people had traveled back to the human realm separately from the contestants. Emotions welled in me, surprising me with their intensity. Ben had been there for the hardest week of my life, and it was only now that we were both out, both safe, that I realized just how much his presence had comforted me.

"Hi, Jacq," he said awkwardly as I flung myself into his arms.

"It's so good to see you."

He held me tightly and the stress I'd been feeling since we returned to Hennington House melted away. Orin was my partner in the FFR, but Ben was my friend.

"Come in," I invited, untangling myself from him. "When did you get here?"

"We left Faerwild just before the contestants did, but the producers took us all out for a meal and put us up for a night in a trendy hotel in Cardiff. Jacq..." He looked me up and down and surveyed the detritus in the room. "Did you know you're covered in dirt?"

"It's a long story." I brushed my face off again and pulled my hair from its ponytail, doing my best to shake it out.

"I won't ask." He grinned.

"I think that's best."

"You all healed up? Ready for round two?"

"Hell, no," I said, shaking my head. "I haven't even been able to sleep. It's all churning in my head. I keep remembering the endless cave and the Erl-king chasing us, and just as I think I'm on the edge of sleep, the dragon pops into my head, and I'm wide awake again."

Ben plopped himself on the bed, a serious expression on his face. "I'm sorry. I can imagine. I was safe the whole time, thanks to all the protective enchantments they put on me, but there were times I nearly shit myself out of fear. I'm not so sure you should go back in."

I looked across at him in surprise. "I've got to go back in. You know that."

"Why? Seriously, why do you have to go back in? There's no law that says you have to. It's only a stupid TV show. Is it about the money? Because I'm not sure any amount of money is worth risking your life for."

He spoke so earnestly I could feel myself being swayed. He had a point—Genevieve and Zee had never made it back from Faerwild. But I wasn't doing it for the money. I was doing it for something much more precious. The Faerie king's Boon. I needed to win to get Cass back, and if I didn't win, I fully intended to stay in Faerwild until I found her. One way or another, I was leaving the faerie realm with my sister.

Unfortunately, I couldn't articulate any of this to Ben. He

didn't know about Cass, or at least, he didn't know more than the few bits he overheard when I was telling Orin. He definitely didn't know that I had a letter from Cass hidden right under where he was sitting. No one knew about it but me. Not even Orin.

"Think of everything I could do with a million dollars," I said, trying to sound enthusiastic. "I'd never have to work again...or you know, living in L.A., I could buy a few cups of coffee!"

Ben laughed at the joke before growing serious again. "I thought it would be fun, you know, a bit of a laugh, a bit of danger...but it's not what I expected at all. They are paying me really well, but..."

"But?" I raised my eyebrows.

"I knew I'd be safe in there, but I wasn't prepared for the emotional stress. There were so many times I wanted to jump in and save you, but I knew that if I did, you'd be disqualified and then you'd hate me forever."

"Are you thinking of quitting?" I asked. I tried to keep the panic from my voice at the thought of being in there without him. Though we'd been able to say so little, he'd been a comforting presence every step of the way.

Ben shook his head. "There's no way I'd let you go in there alone."

Relief flooded me. I scooted closer to him and hugged him again. "You're a good friend, Ben. I'm glad you're my camera guy."

"Me too."

"Feel free to sneak me more protein bars at any time," I said. Suddenly, I had realized how close we were, sitting side by side on the bed. I pushed to my feet.

"Noted." He stood as well.

"Is that why you came to see me?" I asked. "Just to chat and tell me I'm a colossal idiot if I go back over the Hedge?"

"Actually, no. And I don't think you're a colossal idiot. You're just braver than any person has a right to be."

"That's what Orin said," I grumbled.

"The guy does know a few things," Ben said grudgingly. "But I came to get you. There's a breakfast meeting in the dining hall in ten minutes."

Breakfast? I must have been working on my magic longer than I thought. I grabbed my thin jacket from a chair where I'd thrown it, beckoned Ben, and together we headed out the door, leaving the mess of dirt and fern behind.

The dining room was packed, leaving very little room to sit down. At the front of the room stood Gabe, Evaline, and unfortunately, Patricia. She regarded me with a sickening smile on her face as I searched the tables to find a place to sit. Ben had settled down near the back with the other camera people.

I, on the other hand, would have to pick my way through the crowded room until I found a seat. And then I saw him. Orin. My heart leapt as I saw he had an empty chair next to him. As I made my way around the tables, I reflected on how much things had changed since I'd left Hennington House the first time. Before entering the race, I'd have sat literally anywhere to avoid the empty space next to Orin. Now, I was glad that he'd saved me a seat. Like it or not, Orin had become my only ally in the FFR, and he was the closest thing I had to a friend in Faerwild. He gave me a smile as I eased myself into the chair beside him.

"Welcome, everyone, and to our contestants, welcome back," Gabe said, his arms crossed and his feet spread as though he was about to send us into training. "I know you're all hungry and waiting for your breakfast, so I'll keep this brief. I want to let you know how proud I am of you all. I couldn't go into Faerwild, but you can bet I watched every second of it on TV. You all worked so hard to come through, and I know you'll kill it in the next trial. Of course, not everyone made it through. Yael and Duncan used their rings to get out as you know. They're both back home with their families, and last I heard, they were negotiating sponsorship deals with advertisers. That's what you can expect when you come back through. You won't have seen the coverage, but the FFR is huge over here. Ratings have skyrocketed and like it or not, you guys are famous the world over."

I swallowed hard at this news. Despite wanting to work in movies, fame had never been a motivating factor for me. In fact, I'd like to remain as anonymous as possible. I guess that was a pipe dream. Looking around me, I saw that most of the other contestants were practically salivating at the thought of it. When I glanced back at Orin, he grimaced. Maybe we were more alike than I thought.

"Of course, Yael and Duncan aren't the only team we're missing today. You all know what happened to Genevieve and Zee. It was a tragic accident and the..." I didn't hear the rest of Gabe's sentence because rage filled my head, its dull roar drowning out his words. Yes, Genevieve and Zee had died, but I was convinced it wasn't an accident at all. I wanted to stand up and shout the truth to everyone—their rings had been disabled. They'd been robbed of the chance to do what Duncan and Yael did and get out when they were in danger. There would be no lucrative media contracts for Genevieve and Zee. They were gone.

It was only when I felt Orin's hand on my arm that I realized I was shaking.

"You okay?" he whispered, but I didn't reply. I wasn't sure I would be able to keep my cool.

"You have one full day and night to yourselves before you go back into Faerwild for the Elemental Trial, and I suggest you use it to rest. We haven't set a schedule for you beyond mealtimes, but none of you are allowed to leave the grounds of Hennington House. Tomorrow after breakfast, we need you all packed and ready to go back over the Hedge."

A chain of wait staff burdened with dishes were filing into the room, filling the air with the smell of bacon and eggs. Gabe, knowing he couldn't compete with breakfast, gave us a little bow and headed to a table in the corner along with Evaline and a number of FFR staff.

I stood to join the line to get breakfast, but as I did, I noticed Patricia sneaking out of the room. She looked like she was in a hurry. I hustled through the tables, battling the people all going in the opposite direction to get breakfast. I needed to find out what she was up to. I didn't have a shred of evidence that Patricia had anything to do with Gen and Zee's deaths, but my gut told me something was off about that woman. The secret meetings with Niall, the rose and thistle earrings she wore that just happened to be the same symbol as one I saw on the box in the dragon's lair. I was determined to discover what she was hiding—and I had only a day and night to do so.

Unfortunately, it took me so long to get through the crowd of hungry people that by the time I got to the door, she was already gone.

———

I ate until my stomach stretched, and then, I went back for thirds. Orin, on his second helping of pancakes, raised an eyebrow at my plate covered in fluffy eggs, hash browns, and sausage.

"I'm never taking food for granted again," I said.

"We do need to stock up for another week of eating grass and tree bark," Orin said, drowning his pancakes with syrup.

My phone buzzed in my jacket pocket, and my brow furrowed. It was the third time since I'd come down to breakfast.

"You going to get that?" Orin asked.

"I'm avoiding them."

"Who's them?"

"My parents," I said around a bite of sausage.

"Have you talked to them since you've been back?"

I shook my head. I couldn't bring myself to face them. I knew I needed to tell them about Cass, but I didn't know exactly what there was to tell. *Hey Mom, Dad, I think your long-lost daughter is alive and neck-deep in some mysterious faerie conspiracy...* it sounded crazy.

"I know it's none of my business." A pained look flashed across Orin's handsome face. "But...if I could talk to my parents, I definitely wouldn't miss the chance."

I recoiled. "You can't even talk to them?"

He shook his head, looking over his shoulder at Tristam before leaning in. "The king doesn't allow anyone into his palace without a royal invitation. And they're not allowed out."

I glared at Tristam, who at that moment was a fine stand-in for the king. "Dicks." I sighed and pushed to my feet. Orin was right. And besides, I didn't think I could physically fit the food on my plate into my body. I'd overestimated. "I'll go call them."

"Good girl," Orin said.

I grabbed my mug of coffee and walked into the hallway. A cameraperson was standing in the corner, stationed to catch any of us coming out of the dining room. I cut to the left, into the study where Niall once slurred his secrets to me. Not that they had made any sense. Ario and Molly were stationed in the two tall chairs by the fire, leaning in to talk in hushed tones. They turned to look at me as I entered, and I held up my hands.

"Occupied," Molly said, sickly sweetly. I noticed her bubble gum pink hair had changed to bright blue. When she'd had time to re-dye it, I had no idea. My hair definitely wasn't my top priority right now.

"Sorry." I turned on my heel and pushed deeper into the house, searching for a corner away from prying eyes or blinking red lights. Finally, I found a little pantry, filled with shelves heavy-laden with potatoes and jars of pickles and peaches. I sagged against the dusty shelves, wiggling my nose to fight the tickle that threatened a sneeze.

I hit the callback button and tried to calm my nerves.

"Jacq!" My mother answered on the first ring. At the sound of her voice, a lump grew in my throat.

"Hi, Mom," I managed, sagging down a shelf to the cold floor.

"Rick, it's Jacqueline! Get over here. We're going to put you on speaker, honey, okay?"

"Okay," I said, trying to get a hold of the emotions threatening to crash over me. The weight of the last week—the strain of hunger and cold and lack of sleep, of danger and death. Of running for my life. Maybe this was the real reason I hadn't called. Because some part of me had known that with them, I'd have to be real. They could spot my false bravado and determination from a mile away. And beneath that, I was tired, and sad, and scared to go back over the Hedge. I couldn't let myself feel those things.

I cleared my throat and cradled the phone against my shoulder, pressing the heels of my hands to my eyes to hold in the tears.

"Jacq!" My father's voice. "My god, honey, you were magnificent out there!"

"Really?" I asked, looking up. That's not what I was expecting.

"Are you kidding? We're so proud of you!"

"I guess I did kill that panther," I said, a little smile creeping onto my face. "That musta looked pretty cool."

"The panther, what about the dragon!" my dad boomed. "Doing Montana proud!"

At the mention of Montana, my smile dimmed. "How's everyone doing about Genevieve?" Genevieve, the other contestant who had died, was from my same small town.

"The town's in mourning, the tribe especially. How tragic," my mom said. "I know it's selfish to say, but I'm just glad you're safe."

"Me too," I said.

Mom continued. "Dad's proud of all your stunts, but I'm proud of your character, sweetie. You saved Genevieve and her partner in that horrible faerie's house, and you were going to save those idiots who blundered into the Red Cap nest. You never sacrificed your values to get ahead. Hold fast to that in this next leg. Don't let it go."

"And stay away from that blond-haired jackass," Dad added. "He's trying to wrap you around his finger. Don't let him play you. Us Cunninghams know better."

I let out a choked laugh. "Trust me, Dad, I learned that one the hard way. I won't make that mistake again." At the mention of Cunninghams, I knew I needed to ask about Cass. I wasn't ready to tell them what I'd found. Not until I knew more. But maybe they could help.

"Hey, guys, can I ask you something?"

"Of course," they chimed together. God, I missed them. I missed home and the scratchy blanket on the leather couch in front of the fireplace, and my mom's chocolate chip cookies, and the smell of newsprint and coffee in the kitchen in the morning. Why had I not been home to visit lately?

"Remember that old book they found in Cass's room? The leather one with the symbol on the cover? That the ICCF took?"

Silence. "Yes," my mother finally said, the cheer drained from her voice. "Why do you ask?"

"Being here...it's just bringing up a lot of stuff. I thought I saw the same book. I just wanted to know."

"It was called *A Disunion of Worlds*," Dad said. "Not that

they'd let us even get a glimpse at it, the bastards. I've never been able to find a copy. Maybe you can find it over there."

"Thanks. I'll take a look."

"I don't want you to get your hopes up, sweetie," Mom said, ever the practical one. "We did a lot of searching after she was gone." She hesitated. "We didn't want to get ahead of ourselves, so we didn't tell you about much. But...the trail was cold, honey. I don't think we'll ever see Cassandra again."

I had resigned myself to the same fate, but it still hurt to hear it coming from them. Parents aren't ever supposed to give up on their child, are they? But I understood. They had to find some way to live on.

Dad's voice went gruff. "Now you be careful out there. Play smart. Stick with Orin, it seems like you two have a good partnership going. Keep your head in the game. We're not going to let those faerie bastards take another daughter from us."

"Oh, Rick," my mom chided softly.

"They won't. I'll be careful. I plan to win this thing." I felt my resolve hardening within me, my doubts and exhaustion draining away. I wouldn't tell them about my hopes, or the boon—not until I had Cass back. The two of us would come walking up the driveway, and it would be the four of us again. I would bring her back to them. If it was the last damn thing I did.

"If anyone can do it, you can," Mom said.

"That means a lot," I said. "All right, I gotta go. I plan on eating and sleeping as much as I can before we go back in there."

We said our goodbyes, and I hit the red button, cradling my phone to my chest. I had been dreading calling my parents, worrying it would drain my energy and fill me with guilt. Instead, it had buoyed me—given me new purpose. I would do this. I would go in there, kick some faerie ass, and win this thing.

I pushed to my feet, brushing the dust from my leggings. I opened the door, emerging from the pantry into the dark hallway. I shut the door quietly and started heading back when I heard a floorboard squeak behind me.

That was when someone threw a black hood over my head.

3

———

The thick material of the hood darkened the world and muffled all sound. A pair of beefy arms surrounded me, pulling me backward and off my feet. I thrashed in my attacker's arms, my legs flailing uselessly. As my breath came in hot bursts in the hood, I realized I was giving in to panic. As part of my personal quest to make myself stuntwoman ready, I'd taken a couple of self-defense classes at the studio where I did my martial arts boot camp class. Blind panic would not serve you well in a situation like this.

Screaming was my first option, but whoever had me held his...or her hand clamped over my mouth, not only making it impossible to scream, but also making it hard to breathe. Going limp, I let them pull me a few feet while I tried to calm my nervous system enough to decide what to do. Now that they were carrying my full weight, I'd made it difficult for them. Good. It would make it easier for me to escape if they were already struggling.

The person carrying me was strong enough to hold me

with one arm, but I could tell they were having difficulty moving me. The way I saw it, I had two choices. Either continue doing what I was doing and hope they got tired or bored, or be more proactive and fight. In the end, it was no decision at all. The bodies of Genevieve and Zee flashed through my mind. They'd ended up dead. Someone out there was not against murdering contestants for their own gain.

Remembering my training, I took stock of where my attacker's arms were. One was under my arms, wrapped around my chest trying to both lift and drag me. The other was clamped down on my mouth to keep me silent. Whoever held me was strong, but they'd obviously never attended a self-defense class put on by Master Ishiro. If they had, they would have known how easy it would be to push my arm under his and pull it outward—which is exactly what I did. With my other arm, I punched back, aiming behind my head as hard as I could, hoping to hit the nose.

I certainly made contact with something hard. I heard an *oof* before my attacker let go of me completely. I fell to the floor, the hood still on my head and I kicked out. My boots hit against my attacker's leg as he or she took off. I ripped the hood from my head, gasping in the clean, cool air. My attacker was already gone. Pulling myself to my feet, I took a look around. I'd been pulled into the Hennington House kitchens. The hood in my hand was not a hood at all, but a sack that had once been filled with rice.

The lights flickered on, making my heart leap in my chest. Someone stepped through the door, and I almost took his head off with a karate chop before realizing it was just a waiter. I don't know who was more startled, him or me. My breath was ragged in my chest, but it looked like I'd terrified the kid—he couldn't have been older than eighteen.

"I just came to start prep for lunch," he said, his hands up like I was about to rob him. He was probably wondering why there was a crazed woman in his kitchen poised to strike.

I softened my stance and tried to smile. "I'm sorry if I startled you. I ..." I didn't want to tell him the truth. Not only couldn't I trust anyone in the race, I wasn't sure if I could trust anyone in this house either. He looked like a waiter barely out of puberty, but for all I knew, he was a reporter in disguise or he was working for the Brotherhood, whatever the hell that was. "I don't suppose you saw anyone leave the kitchen just before you came in, did you?"

"Someone bumped into me in the corridor outside, but I didn't see who."

How was it possible he didn't see? "Was it a man or a woman?"

The kid shrugged. "I don't know."

Really? "Were the lights off out there too?"

He looked uncomfortable. "I had my mind on other things, okay?" That's when I noticed the smartphone in his hand. When he saw me looking, he went bright red and slid it in his back pocket, but not before I saw who was pulled up on his screen. It was Molly. So the waiter had a crush on Molly, and I'd wasted my time trying to get information out of him, when I could have been out in the corridor chasing my attacker. It was too late now. Whoever it was, was long gone.

I thanked the kid and headed out into the corridor. As expected, it was empty.

The faint chatter of other contestants echoed through the lower floor of the house, but there was only one person I needed to talk to. Orin. I couldn't help my surprise at my realization that he was the first and only person I wanted to tell what just happened. Somewhere along the line, I'd not only come to trust him, but I'd also come to think of him as a friend. How weird my life had turned out. I would have stayed the hell away from someone like Orin back in L.A. But I wasn't in L.A. anymore, was I. I was in a grand house in Wales where someone wanted to kidnap or kill me...and I had no flipping idea who.

As I knocked on his door, a flutter of nerves tremored in my stomach. My heart was still pumping a mile a minute. I tried to tell myself it was the aftermath of the attack—my fight or flight hormones were still going at full pelt. But part of me knew it wasn't just that. Turning to Orin rather than one of the producers or even Gabe meant that it was us against them—and I didn't just mean the other contestants. I meant everyone. It scared me that there was only one person I could truly trust, and that was Orin. Okay, there was Ben, too, but he was part of the show. He worked for them, and he'd already said they were paying him well. I knew he liked me, but I wasn't sure I was worth losing a nice big fat salary for.

Orin and I were on the same playing field with the same goals. All the same, it was unsettling to admit it to myself. That I needed him. I turned around, suddenly wanting to flee to my own room with the door locked. I shouldn't be here.

Then Orin's door opened.

His ebony hair was mussed, and his chiseled face held a look of concern. Just the sight of him soothed me. "What happened?" he asked, taking in my pinched expression. He grabbed my arm, pulling me into his room before checking the hallway behind me to make sure I was alone. He closed the door behind me and turned the key in the lock.

"No reporters followed me if you're worried that the public might think we're having a torrid affair," I tried to joke.

"I'm actually more concerned about why you have blood all over your face. Sit on the bed. I'll get a cloth."

As he left the room to go into the en-suite bathroom, I checked out my face in the mirror. He was right. My upper lip was covered in blood. The attacker must have bloodied my nose as he clamped his hand over my mouth, and the movement of me trying to escape had smeared it all over my face.

No wonder the waiter guy had looked so startled at my appearance. I was disheveled, covered in blood, and wore a crazed expression that hadn't quite managed to go away. In short, I was a complete mess. Almost like being back in Faerwild.

Orin came back and pointed at the bed. "I said, sit. I'm going to clean you up, and then, you are going to tell me what happened."

Obediently, I headed to his bed and sat on it.

He wiped my face gently. The cloth was warm, but it was nothing to how it felt being looked after so intently. I'd been independent for so long that I'd forgotten how nice it felt to be fussed over.

"Please, tell me Tristam didn't decide to take a revenge swing at you."

I shook my head. The urge to cry threatened to overwhelm me, and I fought against it. I wasn't ready to cry in front of him.

"Who did this?"

Taking a deep breath, I shook my head again. "I don't know. I was hiding in the pantry and..."

"Hold up. Why were you hiding in the pantry?"

Pulling my phone out of my pocket, I showed it to him. It was easier than trying to articulate any words. My nerves were more frayed than I thought they were.

"You wanted somewhere quiet to call your parents?" Orin guessed correctly.

"The pantry was the only place I could find that wasn't filled with contestants or cameras. When I came out into the hallway, the lights were off. Someone put a bag over my head and tried to take me somewhere."

Orin's eyebrows knitted together. "Where?"

I hissed as his ministrations touched my sensitive nose. "I don't know. I got away. I didn't see who it was. I didn't know what to do so I came up here to you."

He drew me into a hug. I stiffened for a moment in surprise; it was so un-Orin-like a gesture. But then I breathed in his herbal scent of sage and mint, melting into him. It felt safe. It had been a long time since I felt safe.

"I bet it was that bastard Tristam!" he said through gritted teeth. "He's a grade A asshole."

"He's also the heir to the faerie throne," I replied. "Don't you think kidnapping is a little... beneath him?"

"Like giving people cursed necklaces or stealing horses?"

I pulled out of the hug and felt immediately colder. "Point taken. I guess it could have been him. Molly and Ario were nearby. They knew I was looking for somewhere quiet. It probably wasn't Molly because the person who took me felt bigger. It could have been Ario, I guess. Or Phillip. But what I don't get is why?"

Orin stood, scratching his chin. He seemed lost in his own thoughts. I watched him surreptitiously as he paced the room. The memory of when I first saw him washed over me.

Standing in the warehouse on the studio lot—looking like some dark avenging angel. Too beautiful to be anything but cruel. He hadn't done much to make me revise my assessment through our month of training—but the first trial had changed things between us. Irrevocably.

Now, when I looked at him, brooding away, everything was different. His appearance hadn't changed—he had the same jet black eyes and too-pale skin, the ethereal beauty about him that was mesmerizing. But I saw more now—his quiet intensity that made you want to dig deeper—to find the hidden depths that were clearly there. His stand-offish persona was a mask to keep the world away. But somehow, I'd been allowed in.

Orin turned to me, and I startled, looking away hastily. "I'm not sure what their aim was. Maybe they see you as a threat and would rather take you out quietly than face you on the racecourse. It could be any of them," Orin said. "I've said it before, and I'll say it again. No one in this whole race is to be trusted. There's too much at stake."

"You trust me, though, right?" I asked softly.

"Right now, you are the only person I can trust, and I'm not about to let anyone hurt you again. Tonight you're sleeping here with me."

I opened my mouth in shock at his words before he continued hastily. "I'll sleep on the floor. You can have my bed."

I wasn't sure if I was disappointed or relieved.

At least, he trusted me. That was something. I trusted him, too, and it was about time I told him the full truth. He needed to know about Cass's letter. Then if anything did happen to me, he could mail it to my parents. They said the trail was cold, but they were wrong. I also needed to tell him about the book, *A Disunion of Worlds*, my father had said it was called. I'd never heard of it, but maybe Orin had. Either way, I was going to need his help.

"Why don't you come with me? There's something I need to show you."

4

———

Orin followed me back to my room. I tried to ignore the flush on my cheeks as we passed a cameraman in the hallway, who turned around to follow us. I hated this place. I hated my every move being watched and analyzed. No wonder reality stars were so neurotic. It wasn't natural, to be watched like an animal in the zoo.

We pushed into my room and I slammed the door in the camera guy's face, all too aware of how this must look. I sagged against the door and turned to Orin, who wore a half-smile on his face. "You know how that's going to look, right?"

"Yes," I hissed as I crossed to my bed to retrieve Cass's letter. "Better than the alternative, that they realize we're on to them." I paused, my stomach dipping as a thought hit me. "Unless you have, like, a girlfriend back in Faerwild who would be pissed..." Orin had never mentioned a girlfriend, but I guess we hadn't had a ton of time to actually talk about what our lives were like before the FFR started.

The grin widened, and his dark eyes sparkled with mirth. "Are you asking me if I have a girlfriend?"

"No. Yes. I don't care," I muttered, feeling around beneath my mattress for where I had stashed the letter. Where was it?

"No, I do not have a girlfriend. And—" he paused. "What in God's name are you doing?"

I heaved the mattress up, exposing the box spring beneath. The letter was nowhere to be found. It was gone.

"Those bastards!" I let the mattress drop with a thump, shoving to my feet. I whirled around, examining the corners of my room, the lights. They had to have a camera in here! That was the only way they could have known I had the letter and where I hid it. Where the hell was it?

I was spinning around like a top and Orin stepped in, grabbing my shoulders gently. "Jacq." He was so close I could see the delicate fringe of his eyelashes. "Take a breath. What's going on?"

I looked up, biting my lip. I pulled Orin into a hug, wrapping my arms around him. He stiffened in surprise, but then melted into me, his arms wrapping around my back in a way that was far too pleasant for my mind to function clearly. "There's a camera in here," I whispered into his ear. "We're being watched. I need to tell you something alone. We have to get out of here. Will you come with me?"

Orin nodded curtly into my neck, his nose brushing the delicate skin there. I shivered and pulled back. No time for thinking about how alive my body felt right now. We had to focus on getting to a place where I could fill Orin in without the producers overhearing. "Let's go."

We hurried through the house into the garden. The weather was cold and blustery, as per usual for Wales, and I zipped my FFR jacket up all the way beneath my chin.

"The gardens are impenetrable," Orin said. "We can't get out this way."

"Niall got in somehow," I said. "Before the race started. I think there's a secret gate."

We reached the spot behind a tall hedge where I had seen Patricia and Niall whispering. "It must be around here somewhere."

"There are no cameras here, Jacq. Isn't this good enough? You can tell me here," Orin said.

I shook my head. I didn't trust this place anymore. I needed to be out—away. "I just need to get away for a few hours," I pleaded. "Before we go back in there and our every move is recorded and scrutinized. Please?"

Orin sighed but nodded.

The Harrington House grounds were bordered by a tall stone wall covered in ivy. I felt along it, looking for hidden doorknobs or seams. From Orin's long-suffering sigh behind me, I could tell he didn't think I would find it. "You could help you know, instead of just standing there like Judgy McJudgerson," I shot over my shoulder.

"Who?" Orin asked as he moved next to me along the wall.

"Never mind." I looked down the stretch of wall, despairing. I'm sure the door was well hidden. We might never find it. Down the grassy lawn, a little cottontail rabbit hopped through the row into the interior of the grounds. And I got an idea.

I closed my eyes, summoning my magic earth bunny. It came easily, as we'd been spending more time together. I guess Orin was right—magic was like a needy friend who wanted you to hang out with them all the time. I nudged the bunny toward the wall. *Find me the opening,* I thought.

I felt the tendril of my magic snake out, feeling and

probing along the craggy stones and ancient mortar. Then I felt it siphon *through* the wall. I gasped, running to the spot. "Thank you," I whispered to the magic. I pulled back a few vines of ivy and found the ancient latch—together with our door to freedom.

"How did you do that?" Orin asked as we stepped through into the fresh air of freedom. It was as if the sky was brighter on this side, the birdsong more vibrant.

"Magic," I said sagely, breaking into a grin.

"Seriously?" he asked as he trotted after me.

"A little bunny told me where to look." Ah, this was good fun, confounding Orin.

His eyes widened as he took in my meaning. "You really used your magic? And...the trick I taught you?"

"I've been practicing."

"Good girl," he nodded, impressed. His approval pleased me more than it should have.

Orin and I cut across a verdant green field towards a little dot on my phone that professed to be the White Swan Pub. It was only 10 a.m., and the bars in America certainly would not be open, but this was the United Kingdom, where Guinness was officially a breakfast food.

I was giddy with the excitement of our clandestine getaway by the time we scrambled over another stone fence and into the picture postcard village that held the pub. I took it all in with interest, the tidy cobblestone lanes and the neat brick houses with windowsill flower boxes full of riotous blooms. A red telephone booth stood proudly on the sidewalk, and I burst into a run, pushing into it, turning to Orin with bright eyes. "How do I look?"

"Like a human in a box designed for an obsolete technology," he said, crossing his arms.

I huffed, emerging. "These are iconic. They could never

be obsolete." I stroked the bright red booth for a moment. "I've never been to England before. Or Wales," I admitted as we headed the two blocks to the pub. "I wish I had some time to travel around."

"With a million dollars, I'm sure you can make some travel plans," Orin replied.

The White Swan was everything I imagined a Welsh pub would be. Ancient, wood-paneled walls were plastered with pennants for various soccer (ahem, I mean football) teams, and on the rickety barstools sat a smattering of curmudgeonly patrons who looked like they were regular fixtures. The bartender, a ruddy fellow with muttonchops, raised an eyebrow slightly when he saw Orin and me, but blessedly, said nothing except, "What can I get'cha?"

Orin ordered a lager, and I ordered a cider, enjoying the experience of being of legal drinking age. We took our drinks to a booth by the bright window and tapped our glasses together. "To a successful escape," Orin said.

"Cheers." I agreed. I was feeling about a thousand times better, getting out of that house. I didn't care if we got in trouble later. It was worth it.

"Now, what the hell was under your mattress?"

Reality slammed back to me, and I put my cider down with a thunk. "This is going to sound crazy—"

"Just proceed," Orin waved me on. "Everything about this stupid race is crazy."

So I told him. All of it. The weird happenings before we went over the Hedge. Patricia's rose and thistle earrings, Niall's mention of the Brotherhood, his books disappearing from my room. Seeing the same symbol on crates in the dragon's lair. And most of all, Cass's letter. I was grateful it had been so short; I had every word of it memorized, even though it was gone.

Gen-

Double bad news. We didn't find an MED in Caerleon. Doesn't mean it's not there. Worse, there's been a break-in at HQ. We've had to move. It means you could be compromised. We know the Brotherhood has infiltrated the FFR. Be careful.

-Cass

"You're sure it was from her?" Orin asked.

"I would stake my life on it. The handwriting, the way she folded the page. It's her. Have you ever heard of the Brotherhood?"

Orin shook his head. "No. But what about the other parts of the message? HQ? That makes it sound like she's part of an organized group. And what's an MED?"

"It is like an IED?" I joked.

"What's that?" he asked.

I paused, trying to remember what it stood for. "An improvised explosive device. Or something like that. It's a bomb. Insurgents make them to blow up U.S. troops in countries like Afghanistan."

"I did think it was weird we had to go through that metal detector before we went back into Faerwild," Orin said.

Oh, yeah. I'd forgotten about that. "There was a book, too. In Cass's room, when she disappeared. The ICCF took it, which I always thought was weird. Have you ever heard of *A Disunion of Worlds*?"

Orin shook his head. "Maybe we could find a copy somewhere."

"We don't have time to order it from Amazon," I said. "We go back in tomorrow."

"I don't know what a South American river has to do with this," Orin said. "But there are bookstores and libraries in Cardiff. Maybe we could find a copy."

I pulled out my phone, and Orin came around to my

side of the booth, sidling up next to me. I was hyper-conscious of the sip he took of his beer. My cider was hitting me a bit hard despite my huge breakfast, and my fingertips were pleasantly buzzy as I tapped my phone.

"Try Cardiff University," Orin said. "They probably have a fae section, since they're so close to the portal at Caerleon." His breath ruffled my hair, and goosebumps pebbled my skin. Damn, I was falling hard and fast. This was bad. I needed to be focused for the second trial. I was sure it was going to be even more grueling and evil than the first.

I navigated into the Cardiff University library catalog and tapped in the name of the book. "They have it!" I squealed in delight.

Orin took another sip of his beer. "Fancy another field trip?"

5

———

Unfortunately, they didn't have Uber in Cardiff, so it was another half-hour before we successfully negotiated with the locals to take us into town. I could tell they were nervous around Orin—I had forgotten how foreboding his presence could be when you didn't know him, with his tall, predatory grace and unearthly beauty. I tried to be extra perky and bubbly to soothe any of their nerves, and I think I came off as a little deranged.

"Do you not drink much?" Orin asked as we piled into the back of some guy's Mini, who had volunteered to drive us for £20.

"Well, not a ton," I said defensively. "I'm not legal yet in the U.S. Why?"

"You're acting strange." He shook his head.

I took a deep breath and tried to center myself, not wanting to explain the true reason for my exuberance. "I'll be fine," I said, looking out the window at the countryside sliding by.

"Look, sheep!" I pressed my nose to the window as we

passed a flock of bushy livestock being herded by a black and white sheepdog.

Orin laughed, a deep rich sound that I realized I hadn't heard much before. I liked it. "You need to get out more."

I shot him a black look, but it was soon followed by a smile. I couldn't get over how good it felt to be away from the race, from the cameras. Just hanging out with Orin. Like two normal people. Or a normal person and a normal faerie, you know.

Buildings sprung up around us, and we made our way through tree-lined streets into the center of Cardiff, to the university. As the driver put his car in park, I had a thought. "Can we borrow your hat for another £10? We'll bring it back when we head back through town."

The guy grimaced but handed it over. I pressed the bill into his hand.

We got out of the car, and Orin looked at the hat in distaste. "Is there a reason you want to give me lice?"

"No one has lice," I said. "And you're way too conspicuous. At least with your ears covered, you can pass for just a ridiculously attractive human."

He donned the hat. "You think I'm ridiculously attractive?"

"For a human," I huffed, turning scarlet at my slip. "Let's find this library."

He didn't even bother to hide the sly grin on his face.

The Arts and Social Studies Library, which hosted the archives and rare books, was a squat, concrete, post-modern building that was nothing like the ornate old Welsh pseudo-castle I was imagining.

We navigated our way through the building into the lower floors, which were filled with dusty old books with cracking leather spines. It took us a few minutes to find it, but find it we did. *A Disunion of Worlds.*

I took the book off the shelf with reverence, stroking its black and red leather cover. "What is this symbol?" Orin asked, looking over my shoulder. It was the same one on the book Cass had. The book that appeared in the mirror realm under the faerie hill. I didn't know why, but my gut told me this was important. "I don't know," I admitted, carrying the book over to a table where Orin and I sat down. "Let's find out."

"Look!" Orin said as I opened the cover to the title page.

I pulled in a breath. There was an image of the rose and thistle that I've seen before. "Arthur McQueen, third Order of the Brotherhood of the Rose & Thistle," I read.

"So that's the Brotherhood," Orin said.

"But who are they? What do they want?" I pondered.

Orin made a little hurry up motion, and I turned the page. We crowded together and started reading.

As we turned the pages, a picture started to form. A history. Our history—that of the human world and the fae. "I didn't know the human and faerie worlds were once combined," I said, scanning the page. "How is that possible?"

"Think about it," Orin said, barely-restrained excitement on his face. "In ancient human stories, faeries feature prominently. As does magic. They co-existed. Magic was everywhere. Magic creatures. Magicians. And then at some point, it just...faded away."

"But it didn't," I pointed out. The book said that there was a group of mortal kings that were frightened of the power of faerie magic. They got together and schemed to banish faeries and faerie magic—quora—from the human world. Their magicians worked a huge spell that banished the faeries and faerie magic—separating the world into two realms—the human realm, Earth, and the faerie realm, Faerwild.

"This explains so much," Orin said. "Faerie circles are the portals where you can cross between realms. Ley lines are where the two realms are anchored together."

"I wonder if they realized that when they banished the fae, they would lose access to the most powerful magic. That the human realm would be almost drained of magic entirely. The magic creatures would die off."

"Probably not," Orin said. "Humans have magic, in the essence of aether, but it's so much less powerful than quora. It was probably an unintended consequence."

"The Brotherhood seems pretty pissed about it," I said. The language of the book was...not favorable towards the ancient magicians who split the worlds, or the new set-up. "Unnatural abomination" seemed like a favorite phrase for the author Mr. McQueen.

"They're working to undo the division between worlds," Orin said, his eyes growing wide. "They're trying to get rid of the Hedge. That's what the Brotherhood wants."

"Okay, whatever," I shrugged. "Some old-timey dudes are feeling nostalgic for the old days. Who cares? What does it have to do with the race? With Cass?" We had found answers, but they only seemed to lead to more questions.

"I don't know what it has to do with the race," Orin said, "but we should care very much if the Hedge is destroyed and the two worlds are reunited. Remember how technology can't operate in Faerie? Electronics totally short out? We have magic to work things there. Reunifying the worlds would plunge the human realm back into the dark ages."

"Not to mention the man-eating plants and stuff," I said, horror growing within me. My time in Faerwild flashed before my eyes. Running for my life. The treacherous nymphs, the terrifying Erl-King and his dancing bonfire of hell, the dragon...humans wouldn't stand a chance if these faerie creatures were set loose. I imagined the dragon loose in Santa Monica...it would be a blood bath. "This is bad," I said. "Isn't it?" A flash of bright light went off, and I blinked, shaking my head.

"Yes, yes, it is," Orin replied grimly. I followed his line of sight to where a gaggle of students stood, snapping pictures of us on their cell phones. Uh-oh. It looked like our covert breakout was just about to get a whole lot more public.

6
___

"**S**hit!" I muttered under my breath. Gabe had said how famous we all were, but I hadn't quite grasped the concept. I reserved that word for the likes of Johnny Depp or the Queen of England. It didn't quite compute that the word could ever be used to describe me.

As I turned my head to survey the library, I saw more people pretending to look at their phones while not so subtly filming Orin and my every move. They weren't threatening, just students who happened across a couple of reality show stars, but thinking back to the camera in my room, it made me feel that my days of having privacy were gone. How did those Hollywood stars do it? All these people watching me was making me sick to my stomach.

"Let's get out of here." I picked up the book, and without thinking, reached for Orin's hand. That was it. There was a collective *oooh* from the students, and those of them who had been subtly and not so subtly filming us now dropped all pretense and practically chased us out of the library, cameras held up to capture our every move.

"Aren't you supposed to check that out?" Orin asked

with a smirk as we slid back into the waiting Mini. He was enjoying his minute of fame much more than I expected. It surprised me. He didn't seem the type.

"I'll mail them a check," I blustered. "I hope the producers don't check YouTube."

Orin raised a brow. "YouTube? Dare I even ask? It sounds rude."

My cheeks colored. "It's a website that shows things that people have filmed. A bit like a TV station that anyone can upload stuff to."

"How very interesting what you humans come up with to entertain yourselves." He didn't sound in the least bit excited by it. "I expect the studio staff have better things to do with their time than watch amateur movies."

"Actually it's mostly videos of cute animals and people falling over," I explained, hoping Orin was right.

He wasn't.

At the main gate to Hennington House, Gabe was waiting for us, arms crossed over his chest, his feet planted wide.

"You two better have a good explanation," he thundered at us as we stepped out of the Mini and thanked our driver.

I felt like a kid again, being lectured for not following rules. I pushed the book further under my coat so Gabe couldn't see. I had no idea who I could trust anymore. I liked Gabe and thought he was a straight-up guy with no hidden agenda, but I'd also trusted Tristam and look where that had gotten me.

"I've never been out of Faerwild before now. I asked Jacq to show me some of the sights," Orin lied. He was remarkably good at it, which unsettled me slightly.

"Really?" Gabe looked at me to confirm if what Orin was saying was the truth. I just nodded my head and kept quiet. I was not so proficient a liar. "What sights did you see?"

"We saw a rather wonderful red box that is apparently for the use of phoning someone in 1986. We also saw some sheep."

Gabe nodded, the muscles in his strong jaw working. "The other contestants don't know you snuck out. I like the pair of you and think it would be a waste to see you leave which is why I convinced the studio to overlook this little transgression. I suggest you get back inside quickly and this time stay put. I won't offer you the same courtesy again."

I ran up to Gabe and hugged him. He was so surprised that he kept his arms firmly around his chest.

"Why did you throw yourself at Gabe?" Orin hissed once we were back inside the house.

I'd hardly thrown myself at him, had I? I was thanking him.

"He went to bat for us. I was grateful...wait...don't tell me you're jealous."

Orin huffed. "Don't be ridiculous." But the thought made me bite back a grin.

Having the book in hand made me feel better than I had in a while. It was a part of Cass's journey which meant I was closer to understanding why she left and where she went. I couldn't hide it in my room, not with the secret camera, so I hid it somewhere anyone could get it, but no one would. The Hennington House library. It was a perfect spot, hidden in plain sight between thousands of other books.

As I placed the book on the shelf, the bell rang, announcing lunch. We'd been out longer than I'd realized.

On the way to the dining hall, I heard whispered voices coming from the study. The harsh tone suggested they were embroiled in some kind of argument. Normally, I'd have walked right past them. My stomach was already grumbling at the thought of lunch, but as I passed, I recognized the voices, and it was a strange combo. Tristam and Patricia. I couldn't hear what they were saying, but whatever it was, they clearly didn't agree. Why were Tristam and Patricia arguing? They couldn't know each other very well. And they came from such different worlds. Patricia with her materialistic pursuit of fame and money and Tristam with his ruthless desire for power and winning. Actually, the more I thought about it, they were like two peas in a pod, but I still couldn't figure out what they'd have to argue about. Maybe Tristam was trying to get a leg up in the next trial?

I opened the study door as quietly as I could, but it wasn't quietly enough. Both turned their heads when they saw me.

"I was just looking for...er..." My face turned scarlet.

"Jacq," Tristam stood up and bounded towards me, a smile on that utterly gorgeous and totally punchable face of his. "I've been meaning to talk to you."

I glanced over his shoulder. Patricia gave me a syrupy sweet smile and a small wave to acknowledge my presence, but I could see the annoyed look on her face that having been interrupted had brought about.

Tristam continued, invading my line of sight. "I'm sorry about...you know."

I turned my attention back to him. It gave me some satisfaction that he still had the black eye I'd given him two days before. It was fainter now and more yellow than blue and purple, but he was still going to need makeup to cover it when we went back in tomorrow.

"I'd love to say I've forgiven you," I began. "I really would, but the truth of the matter is you are a lowlife cretin who's using his daddy's name and power to get on TV, and when that's not enough in the field, you resort to cheating and endangering your competition. So really, calling you a lowlife cretin is insulting to the cretins."

His charming smile held, but only just. I saw the hint of a grimace begin to form. He held his hands up. "Well, I hardly think…"

"We already know you hardly think," said a voice from behind me, cutting him off. It was Orin.

"Is everything alright here?" He placed his hand on my back. It was his way of letting me know I was all right. And I was all right. More than all right. "I'm fine. Let's go to lunch."

Tristam's facade dropped completely as I let Orin guide me from the room.

"What was that all about?" Orin whispered as we entered the dining hall and found ourselves a place to sit.

I shrugged. "I don't know. Tristam and Patricia were arguing, but they shut up when they saw me. It just…made me suspicious. I'm probably letting my imagination run away with me. It's probably nothing."

Orin shook his head. "I'm not so sure."

The FFR team, headed by Gabe, walked up to the front of the room, stopping Orin from speaking further. It looked like we were going to get another speech. Great!

Gabe waited until everyone was quiet before he spoke. "The FFR producers have decided to have a little fun and mix things up a bit for the next trial," he began. The collective groans from the contestants rang out in a chorus around me. What fresh hell were they going to spring on us now?

Patricia, who had strode in from the library after us, obviously couldn't wait because she stepped forward and began to talk, leaving Gabe standing there looking like he wanted to throttle her. I knew the feeling. Patricia clapped her hands together. "Next round you are going back into

Faerwild with..." she paused for dramatic effect while I mentally filled in the gap.

With a diamond tiara.

With a man-eating unicorn.

With a herd of giant tarantulas?

"Another team!" she gasped in delight. "You'll still be with your original teammate, but now, you'll have to work alongside another pair to get through."

My stomach fell to the floor. Suddenly, food was the furthest thing from my mind. Why hadn't I just stayed in that pub and drank my own body weight in cider?

She grinned maniacally as if she'd just told us the most exciting news, but for those of us going in, it was the very worst thing she could have said. Over the Hedge, the only thing more dangerous than the scenery was our competition.

7

I woke early, letting the hot water from the shower scald me into some semblance of wakefulness. It was one of those darkly gray, blustery Welsh days that made you want to wrap up in a blanket and sit too close to the fireplace with a cup of hot cocoa. But instead, we were going back in.

Orin and I had talked late into the night about our strategy. We didn't know who we would be teamed up with, but I didn't trust any of our competition as far as I could throw them. Orin and I would have to stay close and watch each other's backs. For as soon as our "partner" team didn't need us anymore, we fully expected to be double-crossed. Well, we'd just have to do the double-crossing first. It was exactly the type of spectacle the show producers were no doubt gleefully hoping for.

Orin had been working on his conjuring, to get us items we needed in Faerwild. We couldn't go through this trial cold, wet, and weak with hunger. We needed all of our wits about us. That meant securing food and shelter quickly so we could focus on moving forward. As I braided my hair in two French braids and zipped up my FFR jacket, I found myself feeling determined. Almost optimistic. We wouldn't let the race push us around, not this time. Though as I walked down the stairs, the niggling voice in the back of my head whispered to me that once we're over the Hedge, all bets were off.

Gabe was down at the bottom of the stairs, clapping his hands, ferrying us towards the front door where a sleek black bus was waiting. "Breakfast on the go, let's go, let's go." As I went to step into the van, getting rewarded by a stiff gust of rain to the face, I spotted another van behind us with our camera crews. Ben was standing outside. He waved and gave me a thumbs up. Bless that guy.

Inside the van, I was greeted by a sea of hostile faces. Tristam and Sophia took the front row. Her dark hair was curled and coifed, her makeup perfect. Next to her, Tristam looked like a post-Photoshop J Crew ad, and I suppressed my desire to muss up his perfect golden hair.

In the row behind them sat Ario and Molly, her with her dark eyeliner and row of silver earrings, black nail polish, and bright blue hair pulled into two pigtails. She blew a huge bubble in her gum, and it popped, loudly. Ario looked at me like a lion eyeing a wounded baby wildebeest, and I found myself shrinking from him before I caught myself and stood up straight, meeting his brilliant green eyes. Amidst his dark coloring and chiseled features, those eyes were striking, glowing like magic. Even without the carnal power he exuded—he was an incubus, after all—he was breathtaking. I recalled the two black wings like bat's wings that emerged from his back at various points during train-ing. He was a competitor to watch.

Next, I passed Phillip and Dulcina, the only two competitors I thought might be decent human beings (or faeries, as it were), until I saw the video of Phillip trying to burn us to death when we were in the mirror realm under the faerie hill, and Dulcina letting him. Phillip's dark, intricate tattoos snaked around his fingers and all the way up his neck to the edge of his dark beard, which made me wonder if they covered the rest of his body, too. His long brown hair was tousled around his shoulders like he just woke up. Phillip met my eyes easily as if he slept peacefully despite his ruthless actions. Dulcina, on the other hand, looked down at her fingernails, indicating that she perhaps had some guilt about what they did to us. She was pretty as a peach with her vivid purple hair, and her ethereal pale skin dusted with sparkles. She was a Pegasus shifter, and the one faerie I had wanted to be my partner. We would have made a good team.

I slid into the seat and turned to watch Orin come down the aisle to sit next to me. It was funny how it all turned out. I would have given anything that first day to pick *any* partner but Orin. Now I was profoundly grateful he was mine. I guessed my judgment really was shit.

"Ready for this?" he asked me, patting my leg in an encouraging fashion.

I offered a weak smile, but I said, "Hell, yeah," loudly, for the other competitors' benefit. I wanted nothing more than to tip my head onto Orin's shoulder and close my weary eyes. But I resisted the urge, leaning my head against the foggy cold window instead.

Gabe appeared at the front of the bus as a girl sporting an FFR hoody made her way down the aisle with coffee and little sack lunches for us. My stomach rumbled, reminding me that this was the last guaranteed meal I'd have for some time.

"We're headed to the airport, where we'll take a quick

flight to La Roche, France. There's a Faerie monolith there, the La Roche-aux-Fees, that will be transporting you over the Hedge." I enjoyed Gabe's attempt at pronouncing the French names. "This trial will not take place in the same playing field you experienced during the Sorcery Trial. You will be visiting new and unknown areas of Faerwild. Be prepared and race smart. We'd like to have all of you coming back this time."

My mood blackened. That wasn't true of everyone heading up the FFR. Someone had sabotaged Gen and Zee's rings, and we needed to keep an eye out for them. Or Orin and I would be next. Actually, the thought of the ring made me realize something. I didn't have a new one. When we were falling from the dragon's talons, the fact that only one of us had a ring had almost ended us. As unreliable as it might be, I'd feel better if I went in with a ring on my finger —and the ability to call for emergency help if it was a matter of life or death. Though the faerie who had responded when I triggered mine had said I wouldn't get another, maybe I could convince Gabe. He seemed like a big softie, deep down.

The van started to move, and I squeezed past Orin to go up to talk to Gabe. I crouched down beside his seat, speaking quietly. "Am I going to get another ring?"

Gabe pressed his lips together and shook his head apologetically. "The producers talked about it. Everyone is going in only with what they came out of the last leg with. That and the Faerie king's gift." The gift. I recalled the little bottle with two pearls that Vale Obanstone, High King of the Seelie Courts, had gifted me in the hospital. "So I don't get another one? Ever?"

"I'm sorry, Jacq. What you did for Genevieve and Zee was honorable." Something flashed across Gabe's face that I thought was anger. But he reined it in. "But the decision has been made. You won't get another one."

I nodded woodenly and walked back to my seat beside Orin. I pulled up my pack from beneath my seat and pulled out the little bottle on its chain, looking at the two pearls inside. "What do you think they're for?" I asked.

"No idea," Orin said quietly, examining them. He peered at them closely, putting his head right next to mine. I breathed in his scent of pine and earth. It soothed my ragged nerves, just a little.

I threaded the chain around my neck and tucked the bottle inside my jacket. It creeped me out to have something given to me by an Obanstone around my neck once again, but the king had said we needed it for this trial. I would have to put my distaste aside.

"What'd you ask him?" Orin asked.

"I'm not going to get another ring." I tapped the metal on his finger. "We can only take in what we came out with."

Orin grimaced, but reached into his jacket pocket and pulled out a jeweled vial. "Want to take my love potion?"

I recognized the object that the xana had given him after he'd kissed her within an inch of her life. "No, I don't want your ...make-out juice!" I turned away with a huff, but Orin started laughing, and the sound was so startling that it made me look back.

"My make-out juice?" he cackled, holding his ribs. I shoved his arm with mine, trying to hold down the laughter that was bubbling up in me to meet his. "You know what I mean! You're an idiot," I said, turning back to the window.

He settled down next to me, his body shaking in a final bout of laughter. "Yes, but I'm afraid you're stuck with me. For better or worse, I'm your idiot."

Yes, he was.

I ate every last crumb of my breakfast and fell into an uneasy sleep. The trip was over far too soon—the bus ride to the airport, the quick flight across the English Channel, another bus ride to the site where we would head back into Faerwild.

La Roche-aux-Fees was a wooded clearing with a circle of tall stones, topped with others that made it look like a little house. If the house was made of ancient, weathered, multi-ton boulders. I felt the faint magic of the place, and it didn't make me as nervous as it had the first time. Magic was an ally, I reminded myself. A friend. I couldn't be afraid of it anymore. Not and make it through this next trial alive.

Patricia and the camera crews were waiting for us when we got off the bus. Patricia was sporting a chic, fitted, black dress with a jaunty half-cape of blue wool in a faint plaid. I had to admit she looked good. I tried not to think of what fashion trends the show was setting. *Half-capes and dirt smeared with faerie monster goo are all the rage this season!*

They had set up another metal detector, and the competitors traipsed through one at a time, Orin and I going last. After I walked through the arch without beeping, an FFR staff member with little curly horns coming out of her auburn hair passed her hands over me, searching for magical enchantments.

"She's clear," the faerie called to her waiting partner. "No enchantments or MEDs."

I nearly tripped over my feet in my hurry to turn back to her. "I'm sorry, what's an "MED?" I asked, trying to bat my eyes innocently.

"Magical Explosive Device," she said in a flat voice. She was clearly ready for her part of this to be over.

Magical Explosive Device. I took in this new information as I went to stand next to Orin, trying to keep the excitement from my face. I tried to fit this new piece into the puzzle of Cass's note. What was it she had said? *We didn't find an MED in Caerleon.* That was where we'd first gone into Faerie. Why, in god's name, was Cass looking for MEDs? Or Gen for that matter? And why did they think they'd find one?

Orin nudged me, and I came back to reality, honing in on what Patricia was saying. She was announcing our partners. "To the first checkpoint of the Elemental Trial, Tristam Obanstone and Sophia Hernandez will be partnered with Phillip Ryan and Dulcina Silver." Realization dawned on me. That meant...

"Jacqueline Cunningham and Orin Treebaum will be partnered with Molly Rhodes and Ario Lazer." Crap.

Orin and I looked at each other in dismay as the horned faerie waved her hands, opening a portal for us over the Hedge. Apparently, the king couldn't be troubled to be at the start of every trial. Fine by me. If I never saw Tristam's father again, it would be too soon.

My mind and body felt numb as I lined up and grabbed the backpack offered to me, following Molly through the buzzing magical field. There was only one thought as darkness enveloped me. Here we go again.

8

The darkness of the gateway clung to me as I stepped through to the other side. It took me a few seconds to work out why it would be night time here when it wasn't back on Earth. The answer turned out to be simple. We were inside...or *under*...judging by the stalactites on the ceiling.

I waited, not daring to move a foot until Orin and Ario came through. I'd only been back in Faerwild twenty seconds and I was already on edge. This place felt far too much like the weird cave system Tristam sent us into for my liking. The weight of rock above me was oppressive, as if it was pressing down upon me.

I blew out a breath as Orin stepped through and joined me. Our new foursome was the first team in. Tristam and his groupies wouldn't be far behind.

"Let's get going," I said, setting off at a quick pace, knowing the other three would follow me. We had no choice but to stick together. I marched forwards at a rapid clip, through long tunnels that opened up into wider caverns, which then narrowed once again.

Ben practically had to run backward to keep up with me. It would look good on camera, I mused. Decisive. The truth was I was unsettled beyond belief, but I was much more worried about what Tristam and the others would do to us than anything in this weird cave. After about twenty minutes, I started to slow down. We had to have put some distance between us and the other contestants.

I came to a standstill and turned. The three others stopped short behind me.

"I think we need to come up with a plan," I said, folding my arms across my chest.

"You think?" wheezed Molly. I'd forgotten how short she was. Keeping up with my quick strides looked to have almost killed her. Her cheeks were bright red and clashed horribly with her hair.

"Do we even know where we're going? This is what, some kind of mine?" Orin asked. "Last time they gave us a clue. It seems strange that we have just been left to fend for ourselves."

"Maybe we should have been checking out the statues we passed instead of running past them at the speed of light," Molly made out between deep breaths.

Statues? I glanced around me. Molly was right. I'd been concentrating so much on getting away from the other team that I hadn't taken in my surroundings. I hadn't noticed how the natural tunnel had given way to something man-made. Or faerie-made, as it was.

Statues lined the walls, each of them lit with some kind of artificial glow. They depicted creatures unlike any I'd seen before, with bulbous noses and ears, and spindly arms and legs.

"What are those?" I examined the one nearest to me. Even compared to the rest, this creature had a particularly large nose. Unless he had something hidden up there, I seriously doubted he could tell us anything.

"Goblins," Orin said, his fine mouth curved in a frown. "I think this is a goblin mine. We shouldn't linger here. Goblins aren't...friendly."

"Great. Where the hell are we going, though?" I asked.

"This might help," Ario purred, holding up a long tubular object.

Orin took it from him and examined it. "It's a cryptex. Where did you find this?"

If he said it was hidden in a statue, I was going to die on the spot of embarrassment.

"I was handed it on the way in. I was told it was the first clue."

I was just about to ask him why he hadn't shown us already, but I knew the answer. It was because I'd practically run off. But at least we were ahead of the other competitors.

"Look at this," Orin said meaningfully as he passed the cryptex to me. It had a row of symbols along the side. I'd read *The DaVinci Code* enough times to know what a cryptex was—a portable puzzle used to hide a hidden message. God knew how I'd survive this race without pop culture to guide me. I was about to pass it to Molly to take a look when something stopped me. One of the symbols was larger than the rest. And I'd seen it before. It was the symbol on Cass's book. But it was upside down.

"What does this mean?" I asked, pointing to it.

"It's an alchemical symbol. It means to come together," Molly answered, huddling close to me to examine the cryptex. She smelled faintly of bubble gum. "I majored in runes at University, and they use some of the same root symbology."

"Does it change the meaning if it's reversed?" I asked tracing the small symbol with my finger.

Molly nodded, taking the cryptex from me. I hated to part with it, but I didn't want to come off as bitchy with my own teammates right from the get-go. Molly was already mad with me for sprinting off.

"Sometimes, it changes the meaning." She scrunched up her face, considering. "I guess in this case, it could mean pulling apart or fragmenting."

I thought back to the book Orin, and I had taken from the library in Cardiff. It was about severing the fae and the human realms. If the symbol meant fragmenting, that would make perfect sense.

Molly handed the cryptex back to me. "These others are also alchemical symbols. They represent various metals. But I'm not sure how that helps us." She shrugged.

"I thought you majored in this," Orin pointed out stiffly. It took a lot of effort to hold back my smirk.

"I said I majored in runes, not reality show alchemy. There's not a 100% overlap," she snapped.

Orin pursed his lips. "So we know one of the symbols. That gets us nowhere."

But I was examining the device, running my fingers across the cool metal dials. I pushed at one, and it clicked forward, revealing something beneath. Another symbol. "There's another row of symbols here, but I don't recognize them. There's also a hole in the end, but I can't see what you'd put down it. It's way too small for my finger to fit."

I looked up and saw Ario leaning against the wall like a fashion model, watching me closely. My ears reddened. He didn't seem particularly concerned with solving the riddle of the cryptex or getting to the next checkpoint.

Orin took the cryptex and placed it in the side pocket of

his bag. "As none of us can figure this out now, I say we keep on. I think I can hear the others."

We grew still. It was faint, but I could definitely hear someone talking.

This time, I let Molly set the pace. We walked for what felt like hours. Always, the same straight path with the creepy statues that seemed to be watching us as we walked.

Eventually, we came to a fork in the path. It was the first one we'd seen since going through the portal. I turned to the others and cocked an eyebrow, asking which path we should take. Both options looked identical, so in my opinion, it didn't really matter which we chose, but I had to ask. My unease was growing the longer we stayed here without incident. It felt like the calm before the storm. The producers wouldn't allow a day to pass without something exciting popping out at us. And Orin said the owners of these tunnels likely weren't friendly.

"I think we should rest up before making any big decisions," Ario said.

I could have gone on, but I could see the fatigue on Molly's face.

I nodded and looked at Orin. He shrugged but dropped his bag to the floor all the same. He was probably thinking the same as me. Don't rock the boat this early on in the game. We had to at least pretend to work together. I'd learned my lesson in the last trial, though. I wasn't going to trust Molly and Ario.

Orin pulled a sleeping bag from his backpack and laid it out. Inside my pack, I found a sleeping bag just like Orin's with the initials FFR embroidered in blue thread. Just seeing those three letters turned my stomach now, though I supposed it was nice of them to actually give us sleeping bags this trial. It wasn't exactly cold in the tunnels, but the floor was hard, and I'd be glad of something between me and the unforgiving ground. I wondered if the race staff had decided that forcing us to spend so much time seeing to our basic survival needs was monotonous to the audience. Did that mean there was food in here?

As I climbed into my sleeping bag, I checked the rest of the backpack. I'd been so busy trying to put distance between us and the other team that I'd forgotten to see what rations we'd been given. It wasn't much, but again, better than the nothing-burger we'd gotten the first trial. I had two protein bars, a bottle of water, and a bag of salted peanuts. I also had a flashlight, a penknife, and a tiny first aid-kit that was barely worth bothering with. A bandaid and squirt of Neosporin weren't going to help me down here.

"Here," Ario said, conjuring up a blanket. It floated down softly through the air on a bed of magic, before covering me perfectly. "I don't want to see you getting cold. You humans aren't as tough as the fae."

I smiled awkwardly, not knowing quite how to respond. As far as I was aware, faeries felt the cold just as much as humans did, and I noticed he didn't offer a magical blanket to his own teammate.

Ario laid his sleeping bag next to mine, settling down gracefully atop it. He moved with a predatory grace that reminded me of the panther that had almost ended me in the first trial. Deadly, beautiful. "Of course, the best form of warmth is body heat."

My cheeks heated. Was he flirting with me? Or was this some ploy? He'd seen how ridiculously easily I'd fallen for Tristam's charms in the last round. He probably thought I was easy game.

Ario winked at me before lying down and closing his eyes. I couldn't help it, my body buzzed with warmth at his nearness, all the way from my core to the tips of my ears. It didn't matter that I didn't trust him and thought he was probably going to murder me in the most gruesome fashion in my sleep, my body had a mind of its own, and right now it wanted me on full alert about the devastatingly-handsome male lain out next to me.

"I wouldn't worry about getting cold," Orin growled at me. His dark eyes gleamed in the low light, fixed on Ario. The exchange between us had not passed beneath his notice. "The heat from your cheeks should keep us all warm."

Sighing, I lay down. To one side of me was Orin. To the other, Ario. Sheer embarrassment left me indecisive about which way to turn. So I spent an uncomfortable night on my back facing upwards. I made a mental note to sleep next to Molly next time.

9

―――――

I woke stiff and hungry, as per FFR usual. It was impossible to know what time it was—whether I'd gotten a full night of sleep. My pounding head and scratchy eyes told me I hadn't, but the others were already stirring, so I sat up with a groan.

Orin was shoving his sleeping bag back into his backpack with more than a little aggressiveness. I wanted to ask him what was wrong, but I didn't want Ario and Molly to see any fissures in our team that they could exploit. Even though Molly's extra knowledge had come in helpful last night, I didn't like having them with us. It changed the dynamic in a way I wasn't comfortable with, setting me on edge. Of course, that's exactly what the FFR producers had been going for. The teams were clearly getting too comfortable with each other, and so they had to dial up the drama by throwing us all together.

Next to me, Ario sat up and stretched, his hand coming within inches of me. "Morning," he said, his voice a deep growl. His dark hair was mussed from sleep, his eyes hooded. He looked like an actor in a movie waking up from a night of raunchy sex. Mortified by my thought, I bolted to my feet, my heart pounding. Where the hell had that come from?

"Everything all right?" he looked up at me, offering a languid grin. It was like he knew what I was thinking. Faeries couldn't read minds, right? Not even incubi?

"Fine," I said, my voice shrill.

"You're wound a little tight, aren't you," Molly complained, bending over and stretching.

"Just eager to get moving," I said, pulling my water bottle from my pack and taking a swig to cover my nerves. I *did* feel wound tight. It was this place. This cave. I needed the sky, the fresh air. No goblins about to pop out at any moment.

We each ate one of our protein bars, took turns finding a spot to relieve ourselves down the tunnel we'd come through and turned to the task at hand. Figuring out which way we were supposed to go.

"They look identical," Orin said, surveying both options.

Molly was walking slowly around the fork in the road, examining it for clues. "Here!" she said, crouching down in front of the right tunnel. "A symbol."

We crowded around her. Etched into the ground was the largest symbol on the cryptex. The one that meant to join together. "It's gotta be this way," I said.

"Nice job, Mols," Ario said, pulling her into a side hug. She grinned, and I felt a stab of jealousy followed by confusion. I just longed for Orin and I to have such an easy exchange, right? I wasn't jealous over Ario...

My feet were slow to move as the others set off down the tunnel. Ario hung back, falling in step beside me. I tried to ignore how his presence felt like the crackle of magic. Was he doing some sort of spell?

"I was impressed by your performance in the Sorcery Trial," Ario said politely.

I snorted. "You mean you're surprised I didn't get myself killed?"

He let out a little laugh. "You proved surprisingly resourceful. Especially, when you went in knowing so little about magic or the fae."

"I know about that stuff," I protested, though his assessment was accurate. Some of the other competitors had studied these subjects for years. I'd had a one-month crash course that I basically flunked.

"Oh, really? What do you know about the incubi?" he asked.

"Um..." I licked my lips, which suddenly felt parched as a desert. "You..." I didn't know how to articulate what I'd heard. "Incubi...have sex with women in their sleep." Suddenly, I felt very alarmed that he'd placed his sleeping bag next to mine.

He let out a husky laugh. "That is a foul rumor. Trust me; every woman who has sex with an incubus is very awake and very willing. Incubi obtain and strengthen our quora from the exchange of sexual energy. We are great lovers—to attract partners to us. Time with us is prized."

Sweat beaded my brow. Where was a cool breeze when a girl needed one? "Ah, good to know," I said. "I guess I misunderstood."

"Our species have been greatly maligned over the years," Ario said. "By other faeries who are jealous of our particular skills."

"You mean jealous that their girlfriends want to sleep with you?"

"Sometimes." Another chuckle. "What about you, Jacq?"

"What about me?" I asked, my voice pitching up an octave. "Human. Human as they come."

"Are you and Orin...involved?" he asked.

I chewed on my lip. Orin and Molly walked before us about twenty feet, Orin moving with that graceful stride that was burned into my memories. But he held himself stiffly, and were his fists curled at his sides? I knew faerie hearing was excellent. There was pretty much no safe answer here. Not in the least because I didn't know what the real answer was. If I was being honest with myself, I did feel something for Orin. But I had felt something for Tristam, too. And now, my body seemed to be insisting that Ario was pretty great. Maybe I was just a human falling prey to faerie pheromones. Maybe I was hopelessly susceptible to their deadly charms, drawn like a fly into a spider's web. Maybe whatever passed between Orin and me was really gratitude at how many times we'd saved each other's hides.

"Orin and I...it's complicated," I finally offered. Who the hell knew? I needed to focus on getting to the end of this race and finding Cass, anyway, not getting involved with some guy. Any guy.

Ario's response was swallowed by a screech of excitement from Molly. "Look!" she said. We hurried to catch up, entering into a wide room that yawned above us in a soaring ceiling. The room was shaped in a circle, and the hewn rock walls around us were inlaid with doors. I counted them. There were ten.

"Which one do we go through?" I asked in dismay.

Orin pulled the cryptex from his backpack, and when I went to look at it, he turned, showing it to Molly instead. I pursed my lips. Any doubts I had about whether Orin had overheard my and Ario's conversation vanished. Great. Now he was pissed at me.

Molly looked from the cryptex to the room. "Ten doors, eleven symbols."

"Well, the symbol for join together is set off. It's larger. So maybe these ten correspond to the ten doors," Orin suggested. "But none of the symbols appear to match."

"If you move the dials, another symbol appears underneath them," I offered.

Orin cast a dark glance over his shoulder at me, before he and Molly looked closer at the cryptex, moving the symbols.

Ario was leaning against the wall again, examining his fingernails. Was this how it always went with the two of them? Molly doing all the work, Ario just riding her coattails? Typical guy, I thought in my head. He'd probably mansplain it to her after she figured it out and take the credit.

"Oh," Molly said with surprise. "The ones underneath are astrological symbols for the planets."

"Those match the symbols on the doors," Orin pointed excitedly.

I moved in, coming around on Molly's side so Orin wouldn't shy away. "Okay, so which one do we go through?"

Molly shook her head. "I don't know. There's nothing to indicate which we should select."

Ario shoved off the wall and strolled over, holding out a hand. "May I?"

Orin scowled but handed over the cryptex.

Ario inspected it, flipping the dials back and forth, hiding and revealing the astrological symbols below. "It's that one," he pointed to a door to the left with a round circle with a dot in the middle.

"How do you know?" Orin asked, suspicious.

He let out a long-suffering sigh and turned the cryptex

to the three of us. "The alchemical symbols on top represent precious metals. Ancient alchemists believed that each metal also corresponded to a planet. Silver corresponded to the moon, lead to Saturn, etc. The symbols beneath are astrological signs representing the planets as well. But they're all jumbled; none of the top symbols correctly corresponds to the bottom symbol. Except this one." He pointed at the round symbol on the cryptex that corresponded to the door he indicated. "This represents the sun, and this," he moved the dial to reveal the other symbol, "represents the metal gold, which corresponds to the sun. I'm assuming the big symbol for 'joining together' is the clue that we need to find the one that correctly corresponds. Plus, alchemists loved gold. It's a safe bet."

The other three of us fell into silence, digesting his explanation. Damn. I guess Ario wasn't just a pretty face.

Molly shrugged. "Good enough for me. Onward?"

I nodded woodenly, ignoring the little wink Ario shot me, together with Orin's black look after he spotted it. Orin turned and stalked after Molly, while Ario gave a little bow, ushering me forward.

I swallowed thickly. I don't know what was behind that door, but I was half hoping it was a goblin horde. Anything to distract me from the awkward faerie sandwich I'd somehow found myself in.

10

———

My heart thudded as Molly approached the door. Literally, anything could be behind there. What if Ario was wrong? He hadn't mentioned knowing anything about alchemical symbols when Molly was talking about it yesterday. It seemed unlikely that he'd just decided to swoop in and save the day at the last minute... but maybe his own self-interest in advancing was enough.

I didn't trust the show producers either. Even if Ario was right, and he did know what he was talking about, I wouldn't put it past them to stash some monster behind the door for us to contend with. As Molly pushed the thick oak door open, I grabbed my knife from my bag and clutched it in my hand. The door creaked, sending an ominous echo through the cavern.

Orin stood in front of me; I could almost feel the tension in his stance. Just like me, he was ready for anything.

Molly, on the other hand, seemed quite content to just open the door and see what happened. As it was, the room behind the door was a major let down. Mainly because it was completely empty. Some kind of artificial light, more than likely magical, illuminated it slightly, but beyond that, it was utterly unremarkable. No more than a small cave, really.

I stashed my knife back in my backpack, feeling foolish.

Molly made to step forward, but Orin grabbed her shoulder and held her back.

"What?" she snapped, turning back to face him. "There's nothing there. I'm just going in to check."

"Just because you can't see anything doesn't mean it isn't there. I think one of us should go first. What say you, Ario?"

"Huh?" Ario clearly hadn't been listening.

Orin repeated himself. "I think it might be better if you or I venture into the room first."

With any normal guy, I would have been offended that he thought Molly and I weren't up to going into a room first because we were girls, but I understood Orin's reasoning. It had nothing to do with our gender, but it had everything to do with our species. No matter how proficient a human was with magic, we would never be able to feel the subtle differences in the magical atmosphere like a faerie could.

"My pleasure," Ario drawled, strolling towards the door. His body brushed against mine as he moved past, eliciting an involuntary shiver from me. Once inside the cave, he stopped and stood still. It was as if he was trying to feel the magic. To taste it on the air. "All clear," he called out. "You can come in, but I'm not sure there's much point. There's no magic here, and there doesn't look to be much else either. I must have been wrong about the clue."

The three of us piled in after him. The cave was, as I had first thought, unremarkable and small to boot. If the other team came along now, we'd all be squashed in here. My mind took off at the thought of being squeezed in between

Ario, Orin, and Tristam, and I had to take a couple of breaths and severely reprimand myself for not staying on task...again.

A hint of red lit up the walls, and for a second, I wondered if I was blushing so much my cheeks were actually lighting up, but then I saw Ben with his camera following us into the cave. I turned away from him, not wanting my embarrassment on display for the world to see.

"Actually, it's not quite empty," Molly said, picking up something small off the floor. It was a black box, barely any bigger than a matchbox, but made out of wood. It would have been easy to miss in the low light. There was another, exactly the same, still on the floor.

"This must be another clue. One box for us, one for the other team,"

"I'm sure the Faerie king's son doesn't need anything so trivial as a clue. Not when he has his daddy in charge." Ario bent down to pick up the second box, but when his fingers touched it, he cried out, pulling his fingers back quickly. "They put a damn spell on it. Nearly took my fingers off," he grumbled. "I suppose it makes sense. It would be too easy to cheat otherwise."

"I guess you were wrong about there being no magic in here after all," Orin smirked. "That's two for two if I'm counting correctly."

"Actually, if the boxes are indeed the second clue, I was right about the symbols and door."

I was acutely aware that Ben was filming everything. We looked like kids squabbling in a playground.

"Why don't you just open the box?" I said to Molly.

She nodded. Inside was a long thin piece of gold. It was cylindrical in shape and had undulating grooves cut into it. Molly pulled it out of the box to give us a closer look.

"Gold," Ario commented. "See. I told you."

Orin just shrugged. Maybe he'd decided to be the bigger male after all.

"What's it for, though?" Molly wondered aloud. "It sure is pretty."

"I think I know." I held out my hand for it.

Molly handed me the piece of gold as Ben pushed the camera between us to get a closer look.

"I'll need the cryptex too." If I was wrong, I was going to look like a monumental idiot...but if I was right...

Orin passed over the cryptex, with the strange hollow in the middle. The gold cylinder fit the hole perfectly. I had to move it around a little as some internal mechanism fitted into the grooves of the gold. Once it was right in as far as it could go, the cryptex gave a faint click, and another symbol appeared. Next to the gold, another hole opened up. It looked like we had to find something else to fit in it.

"Yes!" someone shouted, sending a deafening echo around the small cave.

I'd have berated them, but I wasn't altogether sure it wasn't me. I passed the cryptex to Ario. He'd figured it out before so it stood to reason he could do it again. "Do you know what this new symbol means?"

He looked intently at me in a way that made my toes curl. There was definitely magic in his stare, and if I wasn't careful, I was going to fall for it. I'd already forgotten the question I'd just asked him.

"Ario?" Orin asked, breaking Ario's stare and giving me some relief. He was watching us closely, in a way that made my skin feel too tight. Man, I needed some air.

"Let's go back into the big room to get a good look. It's brighter out there."

I was sure he could see fine in the low light, but it was

getting a bit stuffy with the five of us cramped in the little cave.

I stepped out first and took a deep breath. The air was still musty, but at least, it wasn't as stifling as the tiny cave. Nine other closed doors waited for us. There must be something else for us to find behind one of them. Like the way out of this joint.

"I don't recognize that one," Ario admitted, peering down at the cryptex.

Crap. If he didn't get it, none of the rest of us would. If only they'd have taught this in eighth-grade chemistry class instead of doing stupid experiments with Bunsen burners that I'd never have to do again.

"Let me see," Molly said, peering over Ario's large shoulder. "I know that one. It's another alchemical symbol. For strength."

"Okay..." Ario said slowly. "We have gold, and we have strength."

"That's really helpful," Orin replied sarcastically, and Ario shot him a withering look.

"Actually, it is!" I said, suddenly getting excited. Thinking about my eighth-grade science classes had brought something back to me. Maybe they weren't useless after all. "Pure gold is soft. A lot of the time it's alloyed with other metals to make it stronger. The piece I pushed into the cryptex almost certainly was."

I closed my eyes, trying to think back all those years. I'd sat with my mother in the kitchen going over and over facts about metals for a test. She'd made little cue cards for me so I could remember all the metals and their symbols. Gold was Au. I remembered that one. If only that was the symbol used on the cryptex, then I might have figured it out myself. I didn't actually know what the difference was between chemistry and alchemy, but there clearly was one. I brought my mind back to the task at hand.

"Maybe we need a metal that can be alloyed with gold to make it strong. What metals are alloyed with gold..." I said my eyes still closed. "Silver, copper, platinum, and...er." I searched my mind for the last one, and then it came to me. "Palladium."

"Palladium isn't any of the symbols on the doors," Ario said, glancing around.

"What about the others?"

"That one is silver," he said, pointing to another door. "I don't see copper or platinum either."

I felt a rush of excitement. I might be onto something. I sure hoped my eighth-grade teacher was watching me now on TV. "So the only symbol on any of the doors that's used as an alloy to gold is silver. I think we need to find a small silver rod like the gold one to fill this smaller hole in the cryptex."

Ario nodded. "I can't come up with any alternatives. The door with the silver symbol is as good as any other. At least, if you're wrong, we can always come back in here and try again."

"Why would she be wrong?" Orin snapped.

It gave me a warm fuzzy feeling inside, knowing that Orin was standing up for me. I had to remember that Orin was my partner in this and Ario and Molly were only along for this leg.

"I guess we'll soon find out," Ario said, heading to the door, but something stopped him. It was a noise. I heard it too. It was the sound of footsteps echoing up the tunnel we'd originally come through.

"Looks like the others have caught up," Orin whispered. "Quick, through the door before they see what we are doing and copy us. I don't like the idea of giving the prince any more help."

But it was too late. Before Ario's hand was anywhere near the handle, someone barreled into the room, and it wasn't Tristam and his team. I'd take ten of Tristam over what now surrounded us. Half a dozen twisted creatures with spindly arms and long noses that looked just like the statutes we'd passed. Except these were alive and baring their wickedly sharp teeth at us. Goblins.

11

———

Orin threw up a shield while the other three of us stood, stunned by the appearance of the goblin horde.

The front goblin, with skin like burnt cracking paper, threw itself against Orin's purple shield with a howl, clawing against it.

"Holy shit," Molly said. "Let's get out of here."

We threw ourselves through the silver door, piling into a tiny cave similar to the one we'd just left behind the door marked gold.

Ario heaved the door shut and the two males worked some magic that seemed to seal the door. The inhuman screams on the other side suddenly quieted, as if they were moving through water.

"It won't hold for long," Orin said, turning around. "Tell me we're in the right place."

"I'm not sure yet," I said, desperate to be right. We'd come in here on my mad eighth-grade science hunch. If I was wrong, and we were trapped in here...

"There's something on the wall," Molly exclaimed, and

we crowded around to examine it.

"It's a silver rod, like the gold one," Ario said. "But it's attached to the wall. Poking out of it. I can't pull it out."

A thunk sounded behind us as if something huge was throwing itself against the other side of the door. Dust rained down above us.

I took the cryptex and slid the new hole onto the silver bar that protruded from the wall. Now it looked like...an oblong door handle. I turned. And nothing happened.

"It's not moving," I said, panic surging in me. I surveyed the wall around the rod, and I could see the faint outline of cracks in the stone. A door. This was definitely the way out. Or at least, *a* way out. So why wasn't it opening?

The thuds against the door were growing faster as if the goblins were working themselves into a frenzy throwing themselves against the other side.

"This isn't going to hold for long," Orin said through gritted teeth. "They're working some sort of magic. Eroding the shield."

Molly shoved me out of the way, kneeling down to try to twist the cryptex. "Nothing!" she said. "We must be in the wrong room."

"We can't be," I said, looking over my shoulder as the frame of the door splintered and groaned behind me. "Why would this be here? It fits!"

"Damned if I know," Molly stood, pulling out her knife and raising the other hand. "But it's not working. And we're out of time."

The door exploded inward off its hinges, and the goblins flooded the tiny space. A stray piece of wood struck the side of my quad, sending me to my knees with a gasp.

Ario blasted one of the goblins with a jet of purple

flame, and it shot back into the main room with a high-pitched keen.

Suddenly, it was a melee of snarling beasts and magical explosions.

I scrambled for my knife, knowing it was my only hope. I didn't have the magical chops to summon in a moment like this. A goblin careened towards me on all fours, its black eyes fixed on me. I had less than a split second to think and then it was upon me, its razor sharp teeth coming for my throat. With a scream I stabbed it, catching it in the neck. Its claws bit into my shoulder as it thrashed, black blood spilling out over me.

With a scream of agony, I shoved the thing off me, feeling its claws rend furrows in my flesh as it went.

I surveyed the room just in time to see a goblin spring onto Orin's back, its claws fixed around his throat. "Orin!" I screamed, but he sent a jet of magic into the creature, and it dropped to the ground, smoking. There were other goblins on the ground, leaking black blood, writhing in pain. Had we won?

I pushed to my feet, my shoulder screaming out in protest, only to hear Orin's voice from what felt like far away. "Look out!"

I turned, and that's when I saw the last goblin—it had shimmied up the wall and now launched itself at me like some sort of horrendous jumping spider.

The breath was knocked out of me as something hit me, knocking me to the ground. But it wasn't the goblin like I'd expected. It had come from the side; its weight was pressing me to the ground.

Molly blasted the final goblin with a jet of flame, which illuminated the cave, throwing light on my rescuer. It had been Ario who had pushed me out of the way. Ario—who was now very much on top of me, his green eyes reflecting the light of Molly's fire in a mesmerizing dance. Ario, who, with his crooked grin and his devastating features, was now examining my lips. And leaning down...

His weight left me in a rush. Oxygen flooded back into me as I gasped in a breath.

Orin had hauled Ario off me and now wore a look as black as those goblins' eyes. He reared back and punched Ario in the face.

"Orin!" I screeched, pushing up with a grimace of pain at the movement in my shoulder.

Ario reared back with a shocked look, his hand to his bloody lip. And then his eyes narrowed. Black wings unfurled from his back with a snap, filling the cave with their presence. He went for Orin, barreling into Orin's chest, throwing him back against the far wall.

"Stop!" Molly and I screamed together. She sent a zap of magic at them, giving them both a brief electric shock.

The sparring males fell apart with a gasp. "What the hell, Molls," Ario glared at her, falling to one knee.

"What the hell yourself! There could be more goblins where those came from. We need to get the hell out of here, not squabble like a bunch of babies. Over her?" She looked at me like a soggy sandwich, and I narrowed my eyes. This was between my partner and me.

I stalked across the space and grabbed Orin's arm, pulling him as far from the other two as I could in the little room, stepping over a grotesque dead goblin body. This was not the time or the place for a relationship talk, but we couldn't go on if Orin and Ario were at each other's throats. "Ario saved my life. Why would you hit him?"

"He almost kissed you," Orin snapped.

"So?" I said, my feelings too mixed up for any other response.

"He's an incubus, Jacq. It's what he does. He seduces women. He's trying to come between us. Tear us apart."

I recoiled. "Is it so impossible to think someone could be attracted to me without some devious ulterior motive?"

Orin hissed. "No. Of course not. But he's fooling you. I can see him clearly. He doesn't care about you. Not the way..." Orin swallowed whatever he was going to say next, his jaw working.

"Not the way what, Orin?" I asked, my pulse skittering in my veins. Was Orin jealous of Ario? Did that mean...

An inhuman howl sounded from the tunnel outside. We all froze.

"Oh, hell no," Molly said and stepped over a goblin carcass to return to the main circular room. She was a strange type of warrior, with her tiny figure and her blue hair in French braids and her cat eyeliner...but I had no doubt she would completely destroy whatever was coming our way.

She raised her hands, and the circular room started to shake beneath our feet. I stumbled into Orin, grabbing his arm for support. Rocks tumbled down from the cavern ceiling, a deafening landslide that covered the tunnel entrance where we'd come from, blocking it completely.

I coughed, waving my hand to clear the dust before me.

Molly turned on her heel and marched back, her head held high. "That should hold them."

"It'll hold us too," Ario said, his wings tucking back into his body. "Because unless we figure out how to work this little silver rod thing, we're trapped."

12

"Let's try this again," I said, perhaps a bit snippily, grabbing the cryptex from Molly's hand without asking. I'd had enough. I'd thought the last trial was bad what with the Erl-King and the Red Caps, not to mention the dragon, but I'd have taken on a whole man-eating forest rather than spend another minute trapped in this room with this lot. Not to mention the fact that a goblin had made a scratching post of my shoulder, which was hurting like hell.

The FFR producers knew what they were doing when they put us together. The tension in the room was stifling, even without the claustrophobia-inducing pile of rocks blocking our only exit. Add in the blinking red light of Ben's camera, which had witnessed my mortifying almost kiss with Ario...and I was ready to be carried off by a goblin horde.

I wanted to kick myself. What was I thinking? Getting involved with another faerie? My mess of a love life—or non-love life as the case may be—had been public enough, thanks to the embarrassment that was my connection with Tristam in the last trial.

Ugh. Tristam. At least, he wasn't nearby. With some luck, the goblins had eaten him. There had to be some justice in the world, right? Shaking my head to rid it of the image of Tristam's smarmy face, I turned my attention back to the cryptex.

The silver rod fit perfectly next to the gold one—we *had* to be in the right place. I could see the outline of a door here, and the cryptex *had* to be the key. So why wasn't it working? I examined it. The rows of symbols were messy, all out of order after our epic goblin battle. I frowned at them. "These two rows of symbols spin around. Maybe we have to align them somehow."

"How?" Molly asked, gazing down at the cryptex.

How the eff should I know? I'm not the one who said she studied runes in college but so far has been next to useless. "I'm guessing there is a pattern here, but I don't know what it is." I smiled at her as sweetly as I could muster. "Anyone else know?"

I looked over at Ario. He had figured out the trick with the metals and planets, but he just shrugged, not even bothering to look my way. He seemed to be brooding from Orin's sucker punch. Great! Our only chance of figuring this out and Orin had punched it.

"Orin?"

Orin took the cryptex from me and began to fiddle with the symbols, moving them around. At least he had bothered to try, not that I was expecting him to do any better than any of the rest of us had.

While he was playing with the cryptex, I took the chance to check the room out. Its only redeeming quality seemed to be that it had a door that was hopefully the way out. Dust from Molly's rockslide hung in the air, coating my tongue and leaving me feeling filthy. What I wouldn't give for a long hot shower. And this was only day two.

I unzipped my jacket and pulled it over my shoulder, trying to get a better view of the goblin claw marks.

"Woah," Molly said, catching sight of my mangled shoulder. "That looks bad."

"Is that your professional opinion?" I snipped.

Orin looked up sharply at Molly's comment, starting to gravitate towards me to look at my wound.

"Keep at the cryptex, Rocky," Molly said to Orin, holding up a hand. "I'll fix her up."

I pulled out my water bottle and took a swig, hissing as Molly's fingers touched my wound. Though they were surprisingly gentle, it hurt like hell, throbbing with angry force. There were just a few drops left in my water bottle, which turned the dust in my mouth into a gritty paste that coated my teeth and made me feel sick. Spitting out a black glob of dirt, I wiped my forehead with the back of my hand. It was hot, and I was sweating.

Ario sat in the corner sulking, his wings wrapped around him. It was amazing how little I found him attractive now that he wasn't focusing his charms on me. It was strange to think that Faerwild held magic of every kind. Even sexy magic. Now *that* was something I wish I could bottle.

Molly had some water left, and she dribbled it over my shoulder, cleaning off the blood. "Think goblins have rabies?" I joked.

"Not that I'm aware of," she said, too focused to sense that I was joking.

"You'll need to get this cleaned as soon as we're to the next checkpoint. But, I think I can pull some of the dirt from it, and soothe the pain. It might hurt a little before it feels better."

She started moving her hands in wide patterns, and I groaned as the pain intensified.

"Why didn't you kiss Ario?" Molly asked her voice low.

I raised an eyebrow. Oh, so we were going to have a girly heart to heart? Just what I needed. "You trying to distract me?" I said through gritted teeth.

"Is it working?" she asked.

"I didn't want to," I hissed back.

"Not many people can resist the charms of an incubus."

"Didn't seem so hard." I turned my face away from her, not wanting to engage. I hate that the producers had put us with other teams for these legs. Orin and I may not be perfect, but at least we'd figured out our partnership. Or, we had during the last trial, anyway. Who cared what I felt for Ario. I didn't even care what I felt for Ario. The truth was, I felt nothing for him. Now that he sat in the corner, refusing to help like a petulant three-year-old, he seemed pathetic. Okay, there had been a moment...literally, a couple of seconds where I'd wanted him to rip my clothes off and ravage me on the spot, but it was the magic. It wasn't real, and I was hardly going to tell Molly that. Even though she was being surprisingly nice to me.

Whatever spell she was performing seemed to take effect, because a cooling wave washed over my shoulder. I sighed in relief. "Thank you," I said, surprised. Maybe I had misjudged Molly.

"Can't very well have you dying on us before we get to the next checkpoint," she said, coming around to face me as I gingerly pulled my jacket back on. "It wasn't real anyway."

"What?" I asked. I was so overcome by how much better

my shoulder felt that I couldn't quite remember what she had last said.

"You and Ario," Molly continued matter-of-factly. "It wasn't real. Ario and I are together. We just had a bet to see how easily he could break you and Orin up."

Red clouded my vision. No, apparently my original assessment of Molly was 100% accurate. "Are you kidding me?" I hissed. "First, I would never fall for a pretentious asshole like Ario, human or fae. Second, there's nothing between Orin and me to split up in the first place." As soon as I shut my mouth, I became aware of how loud my voice had become and how quiet everyone was now.

Molly stared at me, her mouth hanging open. Ario grinned at me, one eyebrow raised, but I didn't give a damn about them.

It was the stricken look on Orin's face that sent my stomach to the floor.

My words replayed in my mind, over and over, and I heard them from his point of view. He must know what I meant, right? Orin had become my friend, my defender, and my confidant, but it wasn't like he'd ever been my boyfriend.

I turned back to Molly, rage boiling inside me that I'd fallen into her trap. "Is this all just some sort of game to you?" Was it the promise of money that did this to people? Turned them into vile creatures that would play with people's emotions?

Molly scoffed. "That's exactly what this is. A race. A game."

"People died, Molly. Any of us could have died in here, sliced apart by a goblin."

She shrugged. "Anyone who couldn't handle themselves in Faerwild shouldn't have auditioned."

My mouth dropped open in shock. How could she say

that? What about Genevieve and Zee and their sabotaged rings? I took in a breath to lay into Molly something fierce, when Orin stalked past me and fit the silver peg into the cryptex, and turned. It clicked as a latch freed. He opened the door, and a blast of delicious clean air hit me.

His expression was dark as a thundercloud as he stepped through the door into the light without a glance back at me.

Molly smirked at me as she followed him through. I guess she and Ario had gotten their wish after all. Ario went next, not bothering to be polite and offer me the door first. I was now all alone in the oppressive room except for Ben and his blinking light. I wanted to seize the camera off his shoulder and smash it against the wall, but I was frozen to the spot.

There was no way to go back and yet something was stopping me from going forward. All I had to do was step out the door, but Orin was on the other side, and I'd hurt him. He'd saved my life on this crazy journey and kept me sane in this mad game, and I'd acted as though he was nothing at all.

Still, I had to move. Unless I wanted to spend the rest of my life trapped in this goblin-infested hellhole. I took one last look at the darkness behind me and stepped into the light.

13

I wasn't ready for the barrage of cameras that met us when I stepped onto the lush green grass. The doorway had led to a steeply sloping tunnel that led us up back to the surface. To the first checkpoint in the second trial of the Fucked-up Faerie Race, as I'd decided to call it.

We stood in an idyllic meadow surrounded by stands of tall birches and maples. Brightly colored tents were arranged in a semi-circle around the clearing, reminding me of a renaissance festival.

Orin was already striding across the meadow, toward where, I don't think he even knew. Anywhere away from me, I guessed. I turned on my heel and started off towards the opposite side of the clearing. Anywhere away from Ario and Molly, those backstabbing scheming—

"Contestants!" Patricia's voice trilled, and I turned to see her hurrying across the grass in a flowy marigold dress cinched with a wide leather belt. She wore a pair of over-sized tortoiseshell sunglasses and held a velvet bag in one hand. I knew the race well enough to know that bag probably brought certain doom. She had her camera entourage in tow.

"Contestants." She clapped her hands, motioning for us to gather to her as if we were a bunch of kindergarteners who had wandered off from a circle.

She adjusted her dress and flipped her perfectly shiny curls over one shoulder. "Congratulations on being the first to emerge from the goblin mine." She said it in a spooky voice that made me feel like we'd just emerged from a corny haunted house, rather than an oppressive set of tunnels with vicious faerie inhabitants.

"How will the rankings be decided?" Ario asked, getting right to the point. "Since we came out together?"

"Excellent question. We will be timing how long it takes you to reach each of the three checkpoints, and the team with the shortest time for the three combined legs will be in first place going into the final trial."

Made sense. I wondered how the other teams were going to get out of those tunnels now that Molly had collapsed them. Oh, well. Not my problem.

"I have, in this bag, a gift for each of you that will be integral to getting to the next checkpoint. Who wants to do the honors?" Patricia beamed at us.

It was all I could do to keep from rolling my eyes. Did she think we were excited to head into the next death trap they had dreamed up for us?

"I will," Molly said a bit too enthusiastically for my taste. Whatever. Let her suck up to Patricia all she wanted. I was done with her and Ario too. Molly reached her hand into the bag and pulled out a glittering piece of jewelry. She held it up to the light, and I saw that it was a silver pin in the shape of a set of wings. "Are they all the same?" she asked.

Patricia nodded, shaking the bag again.

Molly handed the pin to Orin, and as it passed from her hand to his, it shimmered slightly. So it was magic. But what was it for?

Molly pulled the next pin out of the bag and handed it to me. It made that same magenta shimmer as it passed to me. I inspected it more closely. Lovely craftsmanship with little amethyst stones in the wings.

"What does it do?" Ario asked.

"Ah-ah-ahh," Patricia cooed. "That's up to you to discover. But you'll start the next leg tomorrow, assuming the other teams arrive at the checkpoint today."

"So until then, we have...free time?" Molly asked.

"Each team has a tent. There's food, drink, a change of clothes, and even an enchanted bathtub!" Patricia sounded delighted. "I'd rest up and get situated for tomorrow."

With that, our briefing seemed to be over. Molly and Ario headed towards their tent, Molly practically skipping, while Orin stalked towards ours.

"Is there a medical team on site?" I asked Patricia.

"Red tent," she trilled, pointing to a far tent.

Good. But my wound could wait. There was something I needed to do first. "Orin!" I called after him, jogging to catch up. As I ducked inside after him, my eyes widened. The inside of the tent was huge, the grass covered with a vibrant Persian rug. Two cots with soft white down comforters and heavenly-looking pillows flanked a huge copper tub against one wall. A polished table and chairs covered in a smorgasbord of food sat in the other corner. Thank god.

"Orin!" I grabbed his arm and pulled him around to face me. His face was dark with soot from the cave-in, but beneath it, his expression was stony. "Are you ...mad at me?" I asked lamely, suddenly tongue-tied.

"Why would I be mad?" Orin spat at me. "There's

nothing between us. We were stuck with each other from the start, no need to pretend this is anything but an obligation."

"Orin," I tried to squeeze his arm, but he pulled his strong bicep from my grasp as if he couldn't stand my touch. "You know that's not what I meant. I meant...there's nothing romantic between us."

"Of course not," Orin said. "You throw yourself at every faerie male that comes within ten feet of you. I'm not an idiot. I'm not interested in being a notch on your magical belt."

My mouth dropped open as my thoughts ground to a halt. Throw myself...every faerie male...magical belt?

"That is so not fair—" I began, but Orin cut me off.

"Why don't you get cleaned up and get your shoulder fixed. You look like a chimney sweep. You want to look your best for the next contestant you need to seduce. I hope we're paired with Phillip and Dulcina next. I mean, he's human, so it's not much of a challenge--"

I slapped him across the face. "Get out," I shouted, feeling tears burning in my eyes. Do not cry, do not cry...

"With pleasure," he shot back, stalking through the flap in the tent.

I stood there in shock for a few moments, my fists shaking at my side. It was so not fair. I had not thrown myself at Tristam. And Ario had used magic on me! And what if I *did* kiss both Tristam and Ario? This was the twenty-first century. I wasn't going to let some backward faerie male slut shame me for being a red-blooded Amer-ican woman...

I let out a scream of frustration. I wanted to throw myself on the bed and pound my fists into the pillow, but it was so downy white, and I was so dirty. So I decided to settle for a bath first. It would make it easier for the medical team to fix my shoulder if I got some of the dried blood off it, anyway.

I figured out the magical enchantments fairly easily (I mean, you just had to turn the knob, and the water appeared) and stood with my arms crossed watching the tub fill. How could I possibly have thought that there could ever be something between Orin and me? We were so different. For instance, he was a moody over-reacting asshole. I was a normal person. As exhausted as I was, I couldn't shake the nervous energy pinging around inside me. I wished I was back home, able to take my frustration out at an ass-kicking MMA class.

Half an hour later, I was reluctant to get out of the bath, as it seemed enchanted to stay warm. But the water had turned grimy and gray, and I knew I needed to get my shoulder looked at. I dragged myself out, toweled myself off, and dressed in a fresh FFR uniform. I was zipping up a clean jacket when Ben ducked his head inside the tent. "Knock-knock!" he said with a crooked smile.

"Come in!"

"Well, that sucked," he said, gesturing a thumb over his shoulder.

I let out a strangled laugh, my remaining tension melting from me. I leaned in and whispered conspiratorially, "I think they're trying to kill us."

"You're doing so awesome, Jacq," Ben said. "Don't be hard on yourself, okay?"

I smiled at him, struggling to hold back tears. The few days' rest at Harrington House hadn't been enough to smooth the rough edges of my nerves. I struggled for a change of subject, anything that felt safe. I picked up the little wing brooch. "Any idea where we're headed?"

"Actually, I have an idea," Ben said, lowering his voice.

"They've been loading all the equipment onto these big sleds. I saw one float up into the air. I think we're going to something high. Maybe a mountaintop?"

My memory of Emerald Mountain flashed before me, and I grimaced.

"Jacq—" Ben hesitated.

"What?"

He shook his head. "I don't know. One of the sleds had some crates that I didn't recognize. I peeked inside when no one was looking..."

I leaned forward. "What was in them?"

"I mean, maybe I've seen too many Bond movies, but..." Ben scratched his head. "It looked like a detonator. Like with numbers or something."

My heart slowed. "Did the crate have a rose and thistle on the side?"

Ben's eyes widened. "How did you know that? What's going on?"

I set my mouth in a line. They searched us all for explosives coming into Faerwild, yet the race organizers stashed some of their own with the show equipment? It didn't make sense. "I'm not sure," I admitted. "But just be careful. Don't let anyone see you snooping around. I need you safe." And I did. Because as of an hour ago, Ben had been promoted to the lead role of the only person I trusted on this whole damn show.

14

I was already in bed when Orin returned from wherever the hell he'd been. I'd visited the medical tent, been healed, eaten my fill of the food they'd set out for us, and finally drifted to the inviting bed.

I closed my eyes when Orin entered, pretending to be asleep as he shuffled around the tent. I could tell that he was trying to keep quiet, but every muffled sound he made set my nerves on edge again. The tinkling of water filling the big bath set my heart racing—part from panic and part from excitement. He was going to take a bath with me right here? He was going to be naked... Well, he'd have to be—I lectured myself. No point bathing fully clothed. And how could I blame him—he thought I was asleep. I was putting on a convincing performance.

I gave what was supposed to be a little snore to show how I asleep I really was, but somehow between my brain and my throat, it came out sounding like a demented warthog. Clamping my eyes even more tightly shut, I sank lower under the duvet and wished for death. Not only was

Orin mad at me; he probably also thought I was now going to spy on him in all his naked glory. Which I was not!

The flow of bathwater stopped, but there was no sound of him getting in. I waited one minute...two minutes. Had he given up on the bath idea? I was so desperate to sneak a peek to see what he was up to, but to do that, I'd have to actually open my eyes. If he caught me, he'd think I was some kind of perverted voyeur who was pretending to be asleep just to catch a peek of her faerie partner. And there was no way that I was going to confirm that he was just another *notch in my faerie belt*. I didn't even wear a belt with these leggings.

It was then that I realized the FFR producers weren't being generous by providing us with some comfort. It was all part of the plan. Get them together; then get them naked. It would make great TV, even if it did come with a content warning. There was no doubt in my mind that there was a camera hidden somewhere in here. *Of course,* the show was filming this. I wondered what the other teams were doing right now. Surely one of the couples must have succumbed to the romance? And it was romantic, I had to admit. The low light in the tents, the fresh scent of the lavender soap, the chance for a full stomach and a warm bed. Not to mention the sense of complete safety from scary faerie creatures that abounded outside. It was enough to make any red-blooded human or faerie horny.

Where the hell was my mind going? I really did need to sleep instead of running a hundred scenarios through my addled brain, each involving the various teams doing things to each other in their own tents. And what it would be like if Orin sat down on the side of my cot, beads of water shimmering in his onyx hair...I banished the thought, wishing I could shoo it away like a fly.

Sleep. I needed to concentrate on sleep. But...Orin still hadn't gotten into the bath. Had he left the tent without me noticing?

Quickly, I flicked my eyes open and shut them again in case Orin was watching me. He wasn't.

He sat on the carpet next to the bathtub, fully clothed, his head in his hands. It was such a different picture from the one I'd had in my mind. He looked broken, defeated, and in that moment, I knew that I was the one who'd caused it. In a moment of anger, frustrated and embarrassed by Molly and Ario, I'd broken the trust that Orin and I had built.

I felt nothing for Ario. I knew that. The animal connection I felt was my body responding to his magic. And Tristam...well, that had been a shallow silly crush that was embarrassing to the extreme.

What I felt for Orin was complicated and beautiful and thrilling, and there was no way I'd ever fully be able to express it out loud. I couldn't imagine the pair of us going for a date to a fancy restaurant, and I couldn't picture us handing over Valentine's Day cards to each other, but at the same time I couldn't...or didn't want to imagine a future without him in it.

Orin lifted his head, and I clamped my eyes shut. This time I heard the sounds of him getting undressed and finally settling into the bathtub.

I kept my eyes closed and let him bathe in peace.

"MORNING EVERYONE, RISE AND SHINE!" The sound of Patricia's shrill voice cut through the remnants of sleep like a foghorn. "Time to get up and start the next leg!"

"We don't even get breakfast?" Orin grumbled as he pulled himself out of bed. He was grumpy and tired, but the sadness I'd seen in him the night before had gone. "Come on, let's get moving."

He pulled on his socks and boots, zipping up his FFR jacket. He stood, walking towards the entrance to the tent.

"Orin," I whispered, but when he turned to face me, I couldn't get any words out. I didn't know what to say. I felt like his black eyes were pinning me to the spot, seeing right through me. "Ario and Molly..." I stammered. "They had a bet. They were trying to come between us."

"And *you* walked right into their trap," he said.

It took all my strength not to shoot back that *he* was the one who was acting childish here. But pointing fingers didn't seem like the best way to get him to forgive me. "I'm sorry," I said. "Ario's an asshole."

"Seems like your type."

Again I stilled my tongue. Boy, he didn't know how true that was.

"I don't want to go into the next leg like this," I said.

"Let's just forget it," he said with a sigh. "Otherwise, they win." Then he nodded his head and left the tent.

That was as good as I could hope to get from Orin. Our fight may not be forgotten, but it seemed we could set it aside for now. He'd at least made eye contact with me, which was a significant improvement from yesterday. I'd take it.

With a much lighter heart, I skipped out of bed, ready to take on whatever crap the FFR threw at us. Before I left the tent, I did a quick sweep of it with my eyes. I didn't see any cameras, but that didn't mean they weren't there.

I was the last to get to the table. It turns out they had laid out a breakfast for us after all. I picked up a croissant and began to munch on it as Patricia stood up before us to announce our new teams.

Not Tristam, not Tristam, not Tristam! I repeated the mantra in my head over and over in the hope that I'd suddenly become adept at thought control or at the very least, wishful thinking. Orin's and my friendship was hanging on a delicate thread as it was. I didn't think that spending the next few days with Tristam would do it any favors.

"Jacq," Patricia said, looking at me as if she were crowning me Miss Teen USA. "You and Orin are paired with Dulcina and Phillip for this round."

Oh, thank god! I'd take the pair that tried to burn us to death any day over my duplicitous mortifying crush and his hostile sidekick. Yeah, I knew I had my priorities out of whack.

Dulcina gave me a shy smile, and Phillip nodded his head in my direction.

Orin came up behind me and passed me a yogurt and a cup of coffee, before holding out his hand to shake Phillip and Dulcina's.

"You have fifteen minutes before the next leg starts," Patricia hollered cheerfully. "Eat your fill."

I hadn't spent a lot of time with this pair, so I was pleasantly surprised at how easily we fell into light conversation. We told them about the goblins, and they made me laugh when they mentioned Tristam falling down a pit in the mines, which turned out to be the goblin latrine. Quite apt as he was always full of shit!

A gong sounded, signaling that our time for breakfast and chatting was over and we had to go back into hell. It was strange—having brunch one minute—then facing unknown horrors the next. I wondered if this is what it was like to be a Navy SEAL or something. Not that I was nearly that cool. Or that capable.

Patricia handed Tristam a piece of parchment before sashaying over to us, handing Phillip an identical note. "Your clue. Good luck!"

Phillip unfolded it, and we all crowded around to read. It was a riddle.

"What passes before the sun yet makes no shadow?"

"Anyone have any idea?" Orin asked, shrugging.

"Maybe it has something to do with these?" Phillip said, holding up one of the winged brooches we'd each been given the day before.

"It's the wind," Dulcina said, looking up, her purple hair shimmering in the sun. "The wind would leave no shadow."

"Okay..." I said. That didn't seem super helpful.

"The sylphs," Orin said, his eyes widening and his face growing pale. "We're going to the Court of the Sylphs?"

But he got an answer as across the field Tristam started to float up in the air. He whooped, doing a little loop-de-loop before jetting into the bright blue. I closed my mouth, realizing I was gawking at the other teams. Molly was looking right at me, and as she floated into the air, she gave me a little salute. That was weird.

"Where do you think they're headed?" I asked, looking around. The landscape was beautiful, with pretty meadows and lush forest around us, fading into jagged cliffs in the far distance. And the sylphs? The word sounded familiar. I felt like Orin had mentioned them before, but I couldn't remember. I'd gotten a bit of a crash course on faerie zoology these last weeks.

Dulcina prodded me in the side and then pointed skyward, up to the face of the tan cliffs. Way, way up.

My jaw dropped again as my eyes adjusted. The tops of

the cliffs weren't just a jagged silhouette as I'd assumed. They were...a castle with soaring spires and bridges. An entire city.

I didn't need to ask how we were going to get up there. The other teams had shown us that much, at least.

I wasn't scared of heights, but the thought of having nothing between me and the ground except a small cushion of invisible magic was enough to make me feel sick.

Ben and the other team's cameraman moved in front of us to catch our reactions. Ben's hands trembled slightly on the camera. I guess heights weren't his thing.

I looked over at Orin, who was staring at the grass, sucking in a deep breath. I remembered how terrified he'd been as we climbed down the mountain in the Sorcery Trial, and how he'd frozen as the dragon dropped us. I hoped he'd accept my help to get him through this.

I held up my pin as I'd seen the others do. Dulcina and Phillip held up theirs too. Only Orin was left. I knew this was going to be difficult for him, so I softly took his hand in mine and raised it, praying he wouldn't jerk it back. Dulcina and Phillip's pins began to glow lightly, and their feet took off from the ground. I waited for a feeling of weightlessness, but nothing happened.

"Come on!" Phillip yelled down to us. He was already ten feet in the air.

"We're trying!" I shouted back, holding the pins up higher. I lowered my voice so only Orin could hear. "I can't do it. I can't do the magic." Shame flooded me, strong and hot. I'd failed. Proven yet again how utterly useless I was at this. But Orin lowered my hand and stared at his pin.

"It's not you. These pins aren't magic. They're as ordinary as something from an old lady's hatbox."

"Why would the producers give us fake pins?" I asked, wrinkling my brow.

"I don't know," Orin frowned.

I thought back to the moment when we'd pulled them out of Patricia's little velvet bag. Maybe there'd been two duds in there and we'd just been the unlucky ones? Molly had pulled each of them out...then handed them to us... hadn't I seen a little shimmer of magic when she handed one to me, and then to Orin?

My eyes widened as I realized.

"What's the hold-up?" Dulcina shouted from above.

"Our pins are broken!" Orin shouted back.

Phillip and Dulcina floated back down to join us.

"They're not broken," I announced, my hands curling into fists at my side. "They've been sabotaged."

15

"What do you mean?" Dulcina asked. "Who?"

"Molly," I said, certainty flooding me. "She pulled all four of ours out of the bag and handed them to us." That's why she was staring at me with that gleeful expression as she took off. Bitch!

Phillip hissed and turned in an angry circle. "Great, so we stumbled into the middle of your turf war with Ario and Molly?"

"They're snakes," Orin spat.

"It's fine," Dulcina said. "We just need to find another way to get you up there."

Orin opened his mouth, no doubt to ask who knew a flying spell that could help us when a shimmer of purple magic lit the clearing.

Dulcina had transformed into her Pegasus form. She shook her downy white mane as she lowered herself onto one knee, clearly offering her back for us to ride.

"I guess there's more than one way to skin a cat," Orin said.

"You guys are so fucking lucky," Phillip grumbled,

shooting up into the air.

I was liking that guy less and less. And I hadn't liked him to begin with.

Dulcina was beautiful in her faerie form, but her Pegasus form was majestic. Her silvery white coat glistened in the early morning light. I had to fight the urge to stroke the feathers of her wings as I climbed aboard, to feel if they were as cotton candy soft as they looked.

Orin climbed up in front of me, threading his fingers in her mane.

"You better hold on," Orin said through gritted teeth, and I threw my arms around his waist with a screech as Dulcina launched herself into the air.

We soared upwards, followed closely by Ben and the other cameraman who were now in some kind of small flying machine. I could see Ben's white face looking out at me through the window. He gave me a small trembly thumbs up, which I reciprocated, as best I could with my hands clutched around Orin's waist.

Dulcina was fast, and we quickly closed the distance between us and the other team. Phillip kept pace beside us, seeming to have turbocharged his little wing brooch some-how. As we soared past Molly, Tristam and their partners, I couldn't resist giving them a wave. Despite the backstab-bing, cheating lot of them, we were once again in the lead.

Orin's muscles were taut beneath my hands, his entire form as rigid as a statue. I wondered if his eyes were closed. If walking on the side of a cliff scared him, he must be terri-fied right now. I pondered what I could do to soothe him, but in the end, I said nothing. Anything I tried to say would be stolen away by the whistle of the cool wind, and I didn't know what I'd say, anyway. Things were still weird between us.

So instead, I tucked my face behind his shoulder out of the worst of the wind, marveling at the landscape passing beneath us, trying not to think of how Orin smelled of herbaceous lavender soap from his bath last night and how hard his abs felt beneath my grasping hands.

The shimmering line of a river snaked beneath us, wending its way between green fields and dark smudges that I knew were forests. I found a grin forming on my face, despite not knowing what would face us when we landed. Once, the most I'd hoped for in my life was my own tiny apartment less than two hours from work and a stunt job on a real Hollywood flick. Never in a million years did I expect that this Montana girl would be clinging to a faerie on the back of a Pegasus, on my way to the Court of the Sylphs, whatever the hell that was, with millions of people tuned in. When I looked at it from that perspective, maybe this wasn't so bad.

We were rapidly approaching the tall cliffs, their stone faces hewn into incredibly intricate arches and windows. It was clear that while the palace sat atop these cliffs, tunnels ran throughout the cliff-face, housing the people of the Sylph Court.

Dulcina caught a slipstream, following Phillip up towards the soaring spires of the palace atop the cliffs. Orin let out a little grunt as our mount tilted upwards and we started to slide backward. "Squeeze with your thighs," I hollered in his ear, not sure if he had spent much time riding. It was all in the legs.

Dulcina leveled off her ascent, and we banked in a circle, heading towards a large open platform inlaid in intricate geometric patterns of different colored rock. While I hadn't dreaded the flight like Orin had, even I breathed a sigh of relief when Dulcina backbeat with her enormous wings and her hooves clattered to a stop on the stones of the sylph aerie.

I slid off her back onto shaky legs—my knees almost giving way. Orin slid off next, and he staggered into me, his face pale and covered in a sheen of sweat. "I'm never doing that again," he said, collapsing to one knee, his palms pressed to the sun-warmed stones.

I hooked my hands under his armpits and pulled him back to his feet. "You're going to have to get down somehow."

"Nope," he shook his head, his eyes closed. "This is my life. I'm just going to live here now."

I patted his back, turning to Dulcina, who had shifted back to her faerie female form. Her cheeks were pink, her eyes bright with joy. "Everyone okay?"

"Thank you so much," I said. "We owe you."

"No problem," she said. "We're teammates, at least for now. Though I think Orin here might have pulled a chunk of mane out, he was holding on so tight." She ruffled her purple locks.

"Sorry," Orin said gruffly as a gust of wind soared over the top of the cliffs, buffeting us.

"The other teams are approaching," Phillip called out, pointing into the distance. "Let's get moving."

We jogged towards him, too happy to get off the exposed cliff-tops that seemed to be designed as landing platforms. "Where are we headed?" I asked, catching up.

"This is the royal palace for the sylph monarchs," Dulcina explained. "The clue led us here, but I'm not sure what we're supposed to do now that we're here. Let's just head inside. I bet there's someone there who will give us our next clue."

"Or something to jump out and try to eat us," Orin said.

"Or that," Dulcina agreed grimly.

I was too busy goggling at the sights around me to worry about any of that as we passed inside out of the bright sun and thin air. The light stone of the cliff soared over us, forming a tunnel with a vaulted arched ceiling. The stone was banded with different colors of tan and pinks, forming a beautiful design.

"What's a sylph again?" I whispered to Orin.

Phillip, who must have overheard me, shot a withering look over his shoulder at me. I stuck my tongue out at him as soon as he turned forward again.

"Air elementals," Orin explained. "Like Zee was a fire elemental. They are close kin to the wind and storms."

"They keep to themselves," Dulcina added, "though the Pegasi and the sylphs have a good political relationship, so I've probably known more than most. They're fairly peaceful, so I'm little surprised they agreed to be involved in the race."

"Guess they couldn't pass up a PR opportunity any more than the next faerie," I said.

"They are notoriously fond of games and riddles," Dulcina explained. "So maybe they were drawn to the logic component of the trials."

We were passing out of the tunnel now into a broad circular courtyard. Over the courtyard stood a delicate latticework of stone that cast beautifully complex shadows onto the stones beneath our feet. A tinkling fountain depicting willowy dancing maidens graced the center, and around the edges were stone benches and flower boxes overflowing with blooms. I thought it just might be the most beautiful thing I'd ever seen.

"Ah hem," a throat cleared behind me, and I finished turning in a circle to find the other three bowing respectfully to a strange male and female standing before us. Crap.

I hurried into a bow as the man spoke. "Rise, fair competitors. Welcome to the Court of the Sylphs. I am King Finverr, and this is my queen, Astra. We are most honored to have you here."

I straightened, taking in the royal pair. They were both incredibly fair, with skin that was almost translucent and curly flaxen hair. The king's poufed in a halo around his head, while the queen's hung down to her waist. They both had thin, angular faces, with wide mouths and striking silver eyes. Their clothing was pastel silk embroidered with threads of silver and gold, the king wearing knee-high boots of the lightest, supplest leather. Just being in their presence made me feel calm—serene, which I knew probably meant I should be doubly on guard.

Footsteps sounded behind us, and I turned to see the other teams approaching, a sour look on Molly and Sophia's face. Tristam and Ario seemed content to ignore the rest of us.

Tristam led with a little bow, which the others followed. "King Finverr, Queen Astra, so good to see you both again. My father bids you hello."

I wanted to gag. Of course, the jerk was playing up his faerie royal status as much as he could. Two beautiful tall women in cornflower blue robes emerged behind the king and queen, bearing trays with glasses of peach liquid. They offered them to each of us, and I took one, sniffing it, trying to gauge whether it was poisoned. It smelled like guava juice.

Most of the others had drunk theirs, so I took a tentative sip. It was delicious, kind of like if an orange and a watermelon had a baby. All I needed was a flower lei, and I could imagine I was being welcomed to some fancy tropical resort.

"Welcome, all of you. This palace is a place of peace and refuge. You will find this leg of the race much different than those of the past. Your bodies have been tested, your endurance, and your magic. Here, your minds will be tested."

The queen stepped forward, her hands opening wide, showing her draping sleeves. "Tomorrow you will face a battle of wits, if you will. But today, we would like to honor you with a feast to truly display the hospitality of the sylphs."

"Thank you," Tristam said, bowing again, and the rest of us murmured our thanks.

The queen continued, "Our valets will show you to your rooms where you can rest and take refreshment. Feel free to explore the aerie. Our home is your home."

With that, we followed the two servants into another hallway. I polished off my juice, dropping the glass in a planter I passed on the way. Orin caught me, rolling his eyes at me. I shrugged. I didn't know where one returned their dishes in a mystical sylph palace.

As we wound through the carved passageways, passing more ethereal sylphs in pastel silks, I pondered this turn of events. Normally, I would consider a fancy party and a test to be seriously preferable to being chased by faerie monsters and trying to survive on apples for a week. But this was Faerwild, where nothing was as it seemed. And hadn't I learned that over the Hedge, the most beautiful things were the most dangerous?

I revised my assessment. The fact that this leg seemed the cushiest of all crystallized one powerful thought in my mind—I needed to be on my guard more than ever.

16

———

I was shown to a room that was so spectacularly beautiful that for a second I thought they'd brought me to the king and queen's room by mistake. I stood at the doorway, afraid to enter.

"Are you sure this is for me?" I asked the valet as I poked my head in and surveyed the rich furnishings. The room was bigger than my whole apartment in Irvine.

"Yes ma'am, is it to your liking?"

"Just go in Jacq, of course it's for you," Orin said, pushing me into the room. I thought I heard him snort before the door closed behind me, leaving me alone in a place that would rival the penthouse in any top hotel. The white walls were painted with intricate murals in pale blue surrounded by moldings of silver that extended right up to the ceiling. The white marble floor was almost entirely covered with the most exquisite rug in swirling colors like a spring sunrise...and the bed...oh! It looked like a piece of heaven itself with a thick white duvet and an avalanche of pale blue and silver pillows nestled against the headboard.

I thought it might be the most decadent and sumptuous

room I'd ever seen, but it was nothing compared to the view the huge windows afforded. Across from me stood a wall of floor to ceiling glass windows, with a long balcony outside that paralleled the full length of the room. Pale blue curtains with delicate silver embroidery hung at each end. It was a toss-up to decide what to do first—run and jump on the bed or head outside to take in the view of Faerwild stretched beneath me. "This is so much better than the goblin mine," I muttered to myself. Finally, the FFR had gotten *something* right. Maybe the viewers were getting tired of seeing us smeared with mud and faint with hunger.

I headed through a glass door to the balcony. The view was, in a word, breathtaking. Below me, Faerwild stretched out for miles. I could see towns and cities and endless expanses of fields and forests. In the distance, I thought I spotted the mountain with the dragon from the last trial, but the view was obscured by white fluffy clouds passing by beneath us. Hearing a noise, I turned to my right. Dulcina was out on her balcony.

"Beautiful, isn't it?" I said in awe. "The view, the room."

Dulcina shrugged. "Not bad."

Not bad? I guess as a Pegasus, she'd seen this kind of thing before, but I wondered what kind of upbringing she'd had where she thought the room only qualified as *not bad.*

The balcony to my left was empty. Of course it was. There was no way Orin would come out, as afraid of heights as he was. I gave Dulcina a little wave and headed back inside.

I had to do it. I just had to. I launched myself at the bed and bounced like a little kid in a bouncy house...and that's when the valet walked in.

"I did knock, ma'am," he said as I hopped, red-faced, to the floor. "I've brought your personal stylist. I thought you might like to have a chat with her about your dress for this evening."

I nodded, trying to keep my face straight as a young sylph female with a sketchpad walked in behind him. "Wait, what dress?" I asked. It was not entirely clear what I would need a dress for.

The female headed over to me. She had eyes as blue as the sky outside. When she spoke, her voice was nothing more than a whisper. "For the ball ma'am. There will be a feast and dancing."

I gulped. The king had said a feast, and I was all about the eating, but I didn't realize we'd have to get fancy.

The valet left, closing the door behind him while the girl looked up at me expectantly.

"Do I really need a dress?" I asked, already resigned to the answer. Wouldn't it be easier and a lot more fun if they just threw us in a pit with a bunch of lions? Certainly less embarrassing for me. I had never been very good at playing dress up. But, I had insisted on wearing my FFR uniform to the debrief after the first trial, and I had ended up feeling super self-conscious. I had learned my lesson. I would let this chick do her thing.

"The ball is the highlight of the sylph season. It just so happens that the Faerie Race coincides with the grand ball this year. You are so very lucky."

"Sure," I murmured, looking longingly at the bed. I guess it was going to be a long time until I was going to get to lie in it.

"So, what do you want? Silk? Chiffon?" Her face lit up. "Oh, feathers are big this year. What style? A-line? Empire? Do you want a peplum? Oh, do you like poufy sleeves? Perhaps a cape?"

I literally had no idea what most of those words meant.

Was she still talking about dresses? A few I recognized though. "No cape. No poufy sleeves!"

She scribbled in her book and began to sketch. "Color?"

I shrugged. Did it really matter? I was here to win a race. "How about you pick my dress?" I said, ushering her to the door. She gave me a wide grin as if I'd just granted her biggest wish and practically skipped out the door.

I sagged with relief when she left, making my way to the downy softness of the bed, my eyes heavy. Last night's cot had seemed like heaven at the time, but compared to this, it was a sad imitation of a bed. A nap sounded like just about the best idea in the world. My eyelids were heavy. Just a few minutes...

A KNOCK on the door startled me awake. I wiped the drool from my chin. I couldn't have been asleep for more than a few minutes. Maybe this was part of the race. Give us all an amazing bed, then keep interrupting us. It was torture. But when I glanced at the clock, I saw that hours had passed. Maybe I had needed the rest more than I thought.

I opened the door to find a longhaired man with a briefcase. He was dressed in a long, white robe which didn't match the black leather briefcase. Frameless spectacles sat on his nose.

It was like Gandalf had decided to become an IRS agent and pay me a visit to audit my taxes.

"I'm here to make you beautiful," he said with a sly smile, pushing past me into the room. He appeared human. I wondered if he'd come just for the trial, or if he lived here?

"Excuse me?" I turned to find him opening his briefcase

on the dressing table. Inside was an explosion of color. It wasn't a briefcase at all, it was a makeup bag.

"Take a pew," he said, patting a nearby chair, upholstered in pale blue brocade. I must have been staring at him with an open mouth because he gestured again for me to come quickly.

His briefcase was like Mary Poppins' bag if it came complete with a never-ending supply of brushes and palettes of color. He put everything to one side and brought out more brushes and products that appeared to be for my hair. I fingered the brittle end of my ponytail and grimaced. A little TLC wouldn't hurt. It's not like I had time for deep conditioning while I was running from dragons and goblins and avoiding double-crossing faeries.

"What color dress did you go with?" he asked as he began combing through the snarls in my hair.

"I didn't. I told the stylist to choose."

The makeup guy snorted through his nose. "Risky move. They like to outdo each other."

I watched my reflection through wisps of hair he'd brushed over my face and wondered what I'd gotten myself into. I'd specified no poufy sleeves, but I'd not thought to tell the dresser that I didn't want any of the dress to be poufy.

"We'll go with diamonds then. Diamonds are classic. They go with anything."

He was giving me diamonds?

I closed my eyes as he pulled on my hair, brushing it this way and that and only opened them when he declared himself finished. I think I dozed off.

When I opened my eyes, I was shocked at the sight. He'd created a work of art. My usual curls had been fashioned into a half-braided updo which he'd decorated with two sparkling diamond hair clips that stuck up in a halo reminiscent of a crown.

"Wow!" I had to admit, I was impressed.

"We've only just started, my darling. Here, put these in your ears." He handed me a pair of diamond teardrop earrings.

By the time he'd finished my makeup, I looked like one of the Hollywood starlets I'd seen around on set sometimes. But more classic and less showy, if I did say so myself. I looked beautiful. My resistance to being dressed up like a doll faded slightly. I guess it wouldn't hurt to try to make myself presentable some of the time. I wondered what Orin would think when he saw me.

"Ah, the dress."

I couldn't bring myself to take my eyes off my own reflection to see the dress, which I assumed had just been brought into the room. I was still so shocked that the image in the mirror was *me*. I never knew I could look as beautiful as I did now.

When I finally beheld it, the dress turned out to be as stunning as the hair and makeup. The sleeveless ball gown was made out of shimmering rose gold fabric affixed with thousands of tiny crystals. When I stepped into it, and it was fastened up, I turned into a fairytale princess.

None of this was my style. The decadent room, the expensive jewelry, the gorgeous ball gown. I was a cowboy boots-wearing, country girl, but right now, just for this moment in time, I'd take it. As I looked at my reflection in the mirror, I could barely see the simple girl from Montana. Before me, stood a princess.

The valet came back to escort me to the ball. As we opened the door I saw Ben standing there, clad in a sharp black tuxedo. His eyes widened as he took in the sight of me, his camera drooping on his shoulder.

"Wow. Jacq..." He shook his head as if trying to clear his thoughts. "Just, wow."

"I guess I need to let faeries dress me more often," I joked. "You don't look half bad yourself." I gestured up and down the length of him. He did look good. His sandy blond hair was combed back neatly, and his shoes were polished to a shine.

"Thanks," was all he said, his cheeks reddening, his eyes still affixed to my dress.

"Aren't you supposed to be...filming?" I joked gently.

"Right!" He hoisted the camera back to his shoulder, his cheeks brightening even more.

I thought I heard the valet snort softly beside me. "Let's go," I said. We strode through the palace, my dress so long that I felt like I was floating. My stomach was aflutter with nerves, and as we stood before the ballroom doors, I had a premonition that everyone else would be in their FFR uniforms and I'd be a laughing stock.

But as the doors opened, I was proved wrong. The room was filled with people in the most wondrous costumes. Women in breathtaking gowns, men in suits of gray and tan, and a mix of strange and wonderful creatures. No one batted an eyelid as I walked through the doors. A couple of very tall faeries with brilliant blue skin nodded at me as the valet left my side, but otherwise, I was just a face in a sea of faces.

The music started up, and the people in the middle of the ballroom began to dance. I headed towards the edge of the room to give them space. The room itself was as beautiful as everything else in this place, with a soaring arched ceiling that was painted to look like a summer sky.

"You scrubbed up well." Sophia sidled up to me looking every inch the Latina supermodel she was. Unlike me with my gown, she'd gone for a figure-hugging eggplant dress that showed off her perfect body and had a split so high up her thigh, I could almost see if she was wearing underwear or not. Her ebony hair was piled over one shoulder, baring her tan swanlike neck and chandelier earrings in sparkling amethyst.

"You look lovely, too, Sophia."

She gave me a broad smile that told me that she knew she was hot shit before she disappeared into the throng, leaving me standing all alone and unsure what to do.

A waiter, or at least, I think that's what it was—it was wearing a white jacket and black pants (though it had four arms and no apparent mouth)—offered me a glass of champagne. Struggling not to stare, and wondering how the hell that faerie ate, I took a glass of sparkling liquid with a smile. I took a sip, grateful to have something to do and some alcohol to take the edge off my nerves. The effervescent liquid was tasty—fresh with traces of a flavor I thought I recognized as caramel.

"You two really should make up."

I turned to find Dulcina beside me. She was wearing a slinky dress in the exact same shade of lavender as her hair, which was piled into an elaborate coif on her head. Her pale skin was covered in sparkles. Not sure if those were natural. But either way, she looked awesome, like a sexy cupcake.

"We did," I replied, assuming she was talking about Orin. "Or at least, I think we did." We'd brushed it under the rug at least. That's about as good as it was going to get.

"He's quite handsome when you get him out of all that black. Sometimes all it takes is a new set of clothes to help you see someone in a new light."

I followed her intent gaze across the room, and then, I saw him. Orin. They'd dressed him in a gray suit with a sheen to the fabric and a slim cut, together with a black skinny tie. His hair was styled in a new way, the layers that had taken to falling into his eyes during the race swept to the side in gelled spikes. My heart stuttered as I saw him. Dulcina was right. He cut a very dashing figure. But that wasn't what made my knees feel weak. It was that he looked as uncomfortable and lost as I felt in this opulent room. "Excuse me for a minute, I've got to..."

"You go, girl." Dulcina took a step back to let me pass, letting out a quiet giggle.

Orin's eyes opened wide as I approached him, his mouth forming the word "Wow." I'd be lying if I didn't admit that the look of awe on his face felt damn good.

"You look—" he said.

"You too," I added, feeling ridiculously shy. This was stupid. Orin and I had been through some serious shit together, we could get through a damn fancy ball. "I feel like a fish out of water," I admitted. "I don't know what to do here."

Orin glanced over my shoulder. "I think we're supposed to dance." He said it like a question, and I nodded. He took my hand and led me out onto the dance floor. My heart hammered in my chest at the feel of his hand in mine and the thought of what we were about to do. We'd been shoved together in close quarters before, but this was different. This was—purposeful. By choice.

As his free arm locked around my waist and we began to move, our bodies pressed together, my heart skittered, and my breathing deepened at the unexpected electricity between us.

Even more unexpected was the way he danced. I would

never in a million year have pegged Orin as a dancer, but he moved beautifully. He spun me around the dance floor with practiced ease, and in his arms, I felt like a pro. As he weaved me around, I caught glimpses of the looks of surprise on the faces of the other contestants. Everyone looked beautiful, but no one was dancing the way Orin and I were. I might have even caught an expression of jealousy in Tristam's eyes. Maybe it was just my imagination, but vindication filled me anyway. Who would have guessed? I was the belle of the ball.

I didn't care about them anyway. I ignored them and the blinking red lights of the cameras. I was here with Orin, and the way he was looking at me through those dark eyes of his filled me with a longing I would never have thought Orin could produce in me.

Everything was in a whirl, and I was falling freely into it. As the song came to an end, Orin lowered his head, his lips moving towards mine. He was going to kiss me. And I was going to let him. It was frightening, and perfect, and a million other things at once.

A flash caught my attention. Just over Orin's shoulder, a girl was racing from the room, her dress bunched up in her hands.

But it wasn't just a girl. It was Cass.

17

I stood frozen to the spot, my feet glued to the ground in my sparkly shoes like they were stuck in cement. My eyes raked over the girl's retreating form. Her blonde curls were pulled into a knot behind one ear, her lean body wrapped in a dress of cerulean silk.

"Jacq. Jacq?"

Orin gave me a little shake. His arms were still wrapped around me, his head tilted towards mine in an almost kiss. "Are you well?" Orin asked, straightening. "You just gasped and went all stiff. You look like you've seen a ghost."

I looked back to the doorway where the girl had just disappeared into the hallway. "I've got to go." I pulled my body from Orin's grasp, hiked my miles of tulle up into my fists, and plunged into the crowd. It was as if the faeries formed a shield before me. Dancing bodies materialized in my way, spinning and smiling. I wanted to scream with frustration as I ducked and wove between them.

Finally, I broke free of the dance floor and had a clear line between me and the door. My heart was in my throat as

I skidded into the bright hallway, squinting against the sunlight.

"Jacqueline!" Before me, in a skin-tight evening gown of scarlet fabric was Patricia, her blonde hair cascading around her bony shoulders. I sidestepped around her, peering down the hallway. It was empty. There was no way Cass could have made it out of sight in the few seconds lead she had on me. Right?

"Jacqueline." Patricia gripped my arm with cold fingers, pulling my attention back to her botoxed countenance. "The king is about to make an announcement about the next leg of the trial. You need to come back in."

"But..." I trailed off, the adrenaline draining from me like a deflated balloon. Had it been someone else? Had my mind filled in a vision of Cass because I longed to see her?

I looked down at my arm where Patricia's perfectly lacquered fingernails bit into the flesh of my arm. A silver ring encircled her middle finger. A rose and thistle, studded with garnet and amethyst stones. That damn rose and thistle again. More Brotherhood jewelry? Just what was a celebrity's connection to a group of stuffy old magicians who wanted a return to the glory days of faerie/human relations?

"You have to go back in Jacq," Patricia repeated, and I didn't have the energy to argue with her. I didn't know why I would. Maybe I was chasing a ghost.

I turned back towards the ballroom, and Patricia let me go with a simpering smile. "I think you're going to like this next leg," she said as if she were my best friend sharing her secret crush. God, I hated her.

I stumbled back into the ballroom, my thoughts foggy and confused. Orin met me by the door, his expression concerned.

"You two don't go anywhere," Patricia said brightly as if we were little kids. I thought she might bop Orin on the nose. "The king and I have an announcement to make!"

"Can't wait," Orin said, rallying a half-decent impression of excitement. "What the hell is going on?" he asked under his breath as Patricia sauntered away.

I swallowed, struggling against tears that were threatening to form. Suddenly being here in this stupid dress felt like a complete waste of time. What if Cass was in trouble? Her letter to Gen had made it seem like they were working against someone—what if whoever it was had gotten to her? I wished more than anything that I could just talk to her. Make sure she was okay. "I thought I saw Cass," I admitted.

"Your sister?" Orin's eyes went wide. "Why would she be here?"

I shook my head, biting my lip to keep myself centered. "I don't know. When I went out to find her, there was no one there. Maybe...maybe I imagined it."

"You all right?" Orin and I turned to find Dulcina regarding me with what seemed to be genuine concern.

I nodded, forcing a smile. "Maybe I had too much of that sparkly wine. I thought I saw a ghost."

A clinking on glass sounded, and I looked up to see the king and queen standing on a raised dais in the corner of the room, Patricia beaming beside them. As pretty as Patricia was, the sylph royalty totally showed her up. They practically glowed with ethereal magic and effortless beauty.

"Would our Fantastic Faerie Race contestants please gather round," Patricia called out.

"Actually," Dulcina said under her breath, as we navigated through the crowd towards the front of the room. "There's less oxygen up here in the aeries. It's not uncommon for a human to see hallucinations. Or have their minds play tricks on them."

Orin raised his dark eyebrow at me. Was it possible? Was my vision of Cass just a hallucination sparked by a tightly corseted ball gown and lack of oxygen? I wasn't sure if that would be a relief or not. Maybe I *was* so desperate to see her that I was imagining things.

The attendees had formed a little semi-circle before the dais, and the eight remaining contestants came to stand in the open space. Ario and Molly looked dashing in matching black, and she shot me a fake smile. Tristam looked like James Bond in a white tuxedo jacket with a vest and tie of gold that complimented his golden locks. He looked annoyingly good in formal wear.

Though, so did Orin, I thought. I narrowed my eyes at the prince and threaded my arm through Orin's.

Orin looked at me in surprise, but then pulled me a little closer, patting my hand on his arm. I was grateful for his steady presence.

"The next leg of the Elemental Trial will be a test of intelligence," the sylph king announced, his voice smooth as silk. "We sylphs are not a people of impressive battles or wild feats of danger. But we are known for our intellect, for our keen logic. To pass through the halls of our court, the contestants will have to best our smartest mind. The Sphinx."

Murmuring voices rose around us, and I looked about, confused. The Sphinx? Like the huge statute in Egypt? Next to me, Orin had paled.

"What?" I whispered.

"It's an ancient creature," Orin whispered back. "Known to guard the most precious of treasures."

"How bad can it be?" I asked.

"If you didn't answer its riddles correctly, it would eat you."

Great. So basically, we're fucked. "They won't let it eat us, right—?" I started to ask, not at all sure that John and the studio execs wouldn't delight in just such an outcome. I should have known that this leg was too good to be true. Us humans were just as easy to kill in a ball gown as an FFR uniform. Easier, actually.

"The Sphinx will present three riddles to the contestants. The first team of four to answer correctly will get a point," the queen chimed in, not to be deprived of her moment in the spotlight. Team of four. So we were still paired with Dulcina and Phillip for the time being. As long as Phillip didn't get near any matches, they were probably my preferred team to be paired with.

"Each question correctly answered will award you one point," Patricia went on. They had this little show choreographed. "If a team of four answers no questions correctly, the Sphinx will present one additional riddle. If you do not answer it correctly, you will be eliminated."

My eyes whipped up at that. What? An elimination round? This wasn't *The Bachelor*! Though, I guess elimination was preferable to getting eaten...

The other contestants were whispering among themselves. Orin and I exchanged a pained glance. I guess the Fantastic Faerie Race was not content to let a leg pass without some sort of drama. Be it backstabbing fae or death by dragon or an ancient faerie beast peddling impossible riddles, they were going to keep their Number 1 spot in the ratings. Orin and I just had to figure out a way to keep our spot in the race.

18

———

Patricia beamed at us, no doubt for the benefit of the cameras trained on the stage.

"Once you have finished your task the feast will be served, so hurry up and get your thinking caps on because we're all hungry, right?" She looked around with a chuckle at the crowd of people who all cheered. No pressure then. Get the questions right and do it quickly!

One of the walls of the ballroom began to move, pulling back so the ballroom was now twice the size. Behind the wall, spotlights shone out, nearly blinding me with their brightness. Patricia stepped down from the dais and beckoned us forward into the light.

As Orin and I were the closest, we were the first to follow. The crowd parted as we snaked through, flanked by cameras. Once I'd passed the spotlight's glare, I saw what I was up against.

The Sphinx wasn't a stone statue as I expected. It was some sort of spirit creature—a magical hologram of shimmering light. The light creature was strange to behold, with the chiselled features of a man, the body of a great lion, and the wings of an eagle. It was formed of every shade of pink and purple, colors that moved in a mesmerizing pattern when the creature itself stirred. The image was so lifelike...it looked real, more than a creature of spirit or magic. I don't know...maybe it was living? I wasn't sure. This was all above my pay grade. At least there was one thing I was fairly sure of. "It doesn't look like it can eat us," I whispered to Orin.

"I agree. I think the real creature is located elsewhere, and this is just its image being projected here. Maybe it's too big to fit in the room," Orin suggested.

That was a relief. The light sphinx was intimidating enough; I couldn't imagine standing in front of the real thing.

Patricia guided us up some stairs to a stage. I navigated them as best I could while hiking up my huge gown and keeping a side-eye on the Sphinx. I didn't trust the thing not to pop out of some other dimension at the last minute or something crazy. This was Faerwild, after all.

I turned once I reached the top and paled, realizing that we were going to have a live audience for this leg. The guests hadn't come just for a ball or a feast; they were here to watch us. My stomach seized. Of course, I knew that the race was being watched by millions of people around the world, but I couldn't see them, so it was easy to pretend they weren't there. This was different. I was keenly aware of the hundreds of eyes on me.

As Patricia lined us up and introduced us all—like we needed any introductions. Everyone knew who we were—the whole place erupted in applause. When Patricia called out my name, I gave a small wave and smile.

The crowd went wild, hollering my name. I tried to gauge the level of the reaction for each of the eight competitors. Not that I cared about fame, as such, but I allowed myself a moment of smugness when the clapping died down a little as Sophia was introduced.

"Now," Patricia began when all the contestants were lined up and introduced. "The test begins."

I'd thought that we'd each take a turn talking to the Sphinx, but I was wrong. The spirit shot right through us like a cold breeze and assembled itself above the crowd. They oohed and ahed at the creature above their heads. I guess it made sense. If it had stayed where it was, the audience would be looking at our backs. This way, they could see the confused expressions on our faces when we didn't have a clue what the Sphinx was talking about.

Patricia explained the rules to us again, as well as the crowd. "You will be able to see the Sphinx speaking, but only our contestants will hear what he has to say, as a spell has been cast on this stage to eliminate cheating. You will, however, be able to hear the answers the contestants have to give, and for those of you that like riddles, I will read them after the question has been answered correctly."

She stepped down, leaving the eight of us to face the Sphinx. Behind the folds of my gown, Orin's fingers found mine. He squeezed once, before letting go. My stomach flipped again, this time from butterflies.

"My first riddle..." The voice of the Sphinx boomed out around me. It seemed to take up every corner of the room and come from nowhere at the same time. It was strange to think

that only those of us on stage could hear what it had to say.

I come in many colors, and I'm rarely on the ground.
It's always very hot, whenever I'm around.

You'll want to run the other way, whenever I'm in view,
But I'll be your best of friends when you have a barbecue.

DRAGON! It was easy. I shouted the word out as a number of the other contestants did the same.

The Sphinx laughed. "My riddles are too easy for you. Yes, you are all correct. The answer is, indeed, a dragon. Four of you answered correctly, but Molly Rhodes spoke first. One point is awarded to Molly's team. "

The four of them cheered and hugged each other.

I furrowed my brow. I'd known the answer. I was just too slow to shout it out. I'd be quicker the next time!

Patricia read out the first riddle for the benefit of the audience who hadn't heard it.

"My second riddle..."

I stood to attention, ready. I wasn't going to let Molly or any of the others beat me this time, and if the sphinx's questions were all as easy, my worries over elimination were definitely unfounded.

WHAT IS A HEAD, *but also has arms?*
What sees over cities, and buildings and farms?
It is hard like a fortress but soft like a glen,
Known far and wide, but not among men.
What has gold on the top and a heart that's the same?
I'm on top of it all, so what is my name?

I STOOD IN SILENCE, not having the first clue what the riddle meant. The sphinx had led us into a false sense of security with the dragon question. This was going to be much tougher than I thought. At least, no one else had blurted the answer out yet. I looked to my right. Sophia had an expression on her face like someone had farted right under her nose, and Tristam didn't look much happier.

"Do you have any ideas?" Dulcina whispered, pulling Phillip and me into a huddle. Orin, to my left, joined us.

"What has a head and arms?" Phillip recited in a low voice. "Doesn't everything? every living thing, at least. It could be a person?"

I shrugged my shoulders. "Not necessarily, lots of things have heads that aren't living."

"Such as?"

"A pin, a piston…"

"A pimple," Orin butted in unhelpfully.

Ew!

"The top and the heart is made of gold. What does that part mean?" Dulcina gave a panicked expression. Time was of the essence, but none of us had the first clue what any of it meant.

"I think it's something to do with the sylph court," I said, reciting the poem back in my head. "We're high up here, so we are on top of it all. That also means we can see over the buildings and farms and whatever. And there's plenty of gold."

"What about the hard and soft part?" Dulcina asked. I could see she wasn't very convinced with my answer. Neither was I, to be honest, but I was spitballing here.

"The wind is soft, but the stone is hard, like a fortress," Phillip answered for me, which surprised me. "And it would be known all around Faerwild, but not on Earth, among men."

I peeked over at the other team who were deep in hushed conversation. If we didn't answer soon, they'd get it.

"It's all we have unless anyone else can come up with anything better?" I was joining Dulcina in her panic. I couldn't be eliminated now, not over a stupid riddle.

Dulcina and Phillip both shrugged, so I looked to Orin.

"It's not the sylph court," was all he said, shaking his head.

"So what is it then?" Dulcina demanded, but it was clear he didn't know the answer any more than I did.

Dulcina held my hand as I walked to the front of the stage. All eyes were upon me as I delivered my answer to the Sphinx.

"Our answer is the sylph court," I said clearly.

"Incorrect!"

The Sphinx's voice seemed louder when he spoke this time, or maybe it was just the added gasp of the audience that amplified it.

Crap!

"We know!" Tristam said, stepping up next to me.

Double crap!

He looked at me and grinned. His smug superiority made me want to punch him in the face. Again.

"The answer is my father. The name is King Vale Obanstone."

That couldn't be right. Heart of gold? Was he freaking kidding me?

"Correct!" the sphinx announced, eliciting another round of excited applause from the audience.

Double, triple, quadruple crap.

"That was a shitty question!" Orin hissed.

I didn't have time to agree because Patricia was already sashaying her way onto the stage.

"Ladies and gentlemen. As one team has yet to answer a question, they are in danger of being eliminated. The score is two points to zero, and if they don't get this right, we might be saying goodbye to some of our contestants."

I felt the pressure in my hand as Dulcina squeezed it more tightly. I didn't know what her story was, but it was clear she didn't want to leave tonight any more than I did.

"My third and final question..."

I closed my eyes. I'd known the last answer I'd given was a stupid answer, but it was no more stupid that Tristam's... and his had been right. I wondered if the king himself had some hand in coming up with the questions—maybe this whole damn thing was rigged. I got the part about the head —he was the head of the kingdom, and the arms must refer to any weapons he had. I saw now that the fortress was stone like his last name, while glen was a synonym for vale, his first name. The gold on the top was obviously his crown, but to say he had a heart of gold? Well, that was pushing it, to say the least. The guy was an asshole of the highest order. Just like his son.

The sphinx spoke, and I stilled my thoughts, listening intently.

*W*HAT WILL NEVER BE *in Faerie but is always in the world?*
What can sometimes be straight and sometimes be curled?
What starts every life lesson and you'll find it in school?
And you'll really want to use it if you fall in a pool.
What the merry fuck?

"Don't you have schools in Faerwild?" Phillip asked, causing Dulcina to shoot him a filthy look.

"Of course, we have schools here. What do you take us for?" Dulcina scoffed.

"It doesn't make sense then. How can it be in a school if it isn't in the faerie realm?"

It was clear that lateral thinking wasn't Phillip's strong suit.

"You've been quiet?" I pointed out, turning to Orin. "Do you have any ideas?"

I certainly hoped so, because I didn't know the answer. Though why had the sphinx called the realm *Faerie*, not Faerwild, its name?

"I'd want a life preserver if I fell in a pool, but I don't see how that fits in with the rest of it," Orin admitted.

Dulcina jumped up. "We don't have life preservers in Faerwild, but you might find one in a school if the school has a pool."

This was beginning to sound like a Dr. Seuss story. "It's not a life preserver," I said, shutting my eyes. I had it. I had something—but whatever thought was in my mind swirled around uncrystallized and refused to come to the front.

"We have the answer," Ario stepped forward.

We all looked up in horror. We were just about to be eliminated.

19

"The answer is human knowledge," Ario said.

My lungs felt like they were going to burst as the Sphinx paused. Stupid reality show drama...

"That is incorrect," the Sphinx said.

I blew out a shaky breath. Oh, thank god. That answer didn't work with the straight and curly clue. They must have been panicking. Like we now didn't have to. I turned my attention back to the problem, and to the thought that had been tickling the back of my mind.

Phillip began, "It migh—"

I shushed him, closing my hand like a trap. I ran the poem through my head a few more times. It wasn't what it appeared to be, and it wasn't a stupid answer like the king.

"I know it!" I grinned.

"Are you sure?" Dulcina asked, "because you thought you knew the last one, and you couldn't have been more wrong." I pursed my lips. Thanks for the vote of confidence!

"I'm sure," I whispered my answer to them and watched as Orin, Dulcina, and Phillip all considered, rolling it through the clues.

"Genius," Orin grinned.

I stepped forward once again and gave them my answer. "The answer is the letter L. It's not in the word faerie, but it is the words world, life, and school. If you don't use it in the word pool, you'll fall in something you'd never want to fall in." The audience laughed as I explained my answer. I held my breath waiting for the sphinx to tell me I was wrong.

"Correct!"

I pressed my hand to my chest as if I could hold in my heart. I'd done it. We were still in the race.

I felt like I had been run through an emotional ringer as I walked back down the steps on shaky legs. The beautiful faces and gorgeous dresses blurred around me, the cheering nearly overwhelming. I was normally okay around crowds, but right now, I wanted to crawl under the covers.

Then I felt a steadying hand on my back and realized it was Orin. "Want to get some air?" he asked.

I nodded gratefully. We snaked through the crowd and pushed out a set of glass double doors onto a wide veranda. The cool breeze stole the flush from my skin, and I sighed even as the goosebumps pricked on my arms. I could finally clear my head.

Next to me, Orin was standing stiff as a board, backed against the wall of the ballroom. "Maybe this wasn't such a great idea."

Oh, yeah. He was afraid of heights. I went to stand before him, blocking his view of the green expanse below. "Just focus on me," I said, putting my hands on his shoulders. "Breathe."

He took several deep breaths, gazing directly at my chest with a glazed expression, his eyes wide with fright. "Better?" I asked.

He nodded.

"Good. I'll excuse you staring at my boobs then," I said.

Orin looked up, shocked, his cheeks reddening. "I wasn't staring at—"

I started laughing, and he rolled his eyes. "I suppose they are preferable to the alternative."

"Plunging to your death?" I snorted. "You flatter."

"Nice job in there," Orin admitted. "The letter l. I never would have gotten it."

"Just did what I had to."

"Well, you did good." It was my turn to blush. I was finding compliments from Orin to be a treasured commodity.

"You know we have Tristam and Sophia as our teammates for the next leg?" I asked.

"If he has a heart of gold like his father," Orin shrugged. "How bad can it be?"

"That question was such bullshit!" I shook my head. "Stupid nepotism."

Orin chuckled. "Ready to go back in there?"

I pulled in a breath.

"There's food…"

I threaded my arm into Orin's, and we turned back toward the door. "You should have led with the food," I said. "That's a strong selling point."

I COLLAPSED onto my bed that night, my feet killing me from the heels, my back aching from the tight dress, my mind still uneasy over my possibly-hallucinated sighting of Cass. But the evening hadn't been all bad. We had actually talked and joked a bit with Phillip and Dulcina, the food had been bomb, and it wasn't so bad having faeries come up to me and ask for my autograph. There were worse things.

But the sunlight spilled through my wall of windows bright and early, and it took all my effort to drag myself from bed. The next leg started today, and after the break we'd been given from death and danger, I had a powerful suspicion that we were about to face something awful.

I showered, brushed my teeth, and went to put on a clean FFR uniform. It would feel good to be back in the functional clothing, even though I knew it meant more dirt and danger and cold nights and hungry days. But when I opened the wardrobe, the FFR uniform I found was new. Different.

I fingered the fabric. It was thick and squishy, like Neoprene. I struggled to pull on the skin-tight bodysuit, my mind racing. When I finally got the silver and blue suit on and zipped it up, I regarded myself in the mirror. It looked like a wetsuit. Crap.

When I walked into the main hall, where a buffet of breakfast food was laid out, I spotted Orin. The guy looked…pretty damn good in a skin-tight wetsuit thingy. It highlighted the muscled V of his torso, his strong legs, his… really cute ass.

"Eyes up here, Cunningham," Orin called from around a bite of muffin, motioning to his face with his two fingers.

I let out a strangled laugh, hurrying over to a three-tiered silver tray laden with strange colorful fruits. "You wish." But my heart wasn't in it. Because I kinda wondered if he wished. And sorta wished he wished, too. I shoved a slice of pink melon into my mouth, wishing whatever watery hell we were off to next would just swallow me up now.

I kept my eyes fixed firmly at eye level for the few minutes it took me to eat, chug a cup of coffee flavored with some delicious nutty creamer, and head out to the wide veranda where we'd first landed.

Tristam sauntered up to us, Sophia in his wake. They both looked annoyingly perfect in their wetsuits, like a couple of Baywatch cast members. What was next, FFR? The swimsuit competition? "Think we're headed under the sea?" Tristam asked, his arms crossed over his broad chest.

"Didn't your dad tell you?" I asked with mock sweetness.

"Tristam hasn't gotten any special treatment," Sophia shot back.

"Of course," Orin said mockingly. "We each had a riddle specially tailored for us, didn't we? Oh wait..." he tapped his chin as if considering.

"It's not Tristam's fault he's the son of the monarch of the entire Seelie Courts." Sophia took a step closer.

"But it is his fault that he's a two-faced, cheating liar," I said, matching Sophia step for step.

"Ladies," Tristam chuckled as if we were fighting over him, and it took all my restraint not to pop him in the nose again. God, the guy infuriated me!

"We're going to need to work together on the next leg," Orin said grudgingly. Patricia hadn't announced it yet, but we'd already been paired with the other two teams. It was a process of elimination. "Let's just put our feelings aside for this next leg. Agreed?"

I chewed my lip but nodded.

"Fine," Sophia huffed.

My attention was drawn by something soaring through the bright morning towards our platform. I squinted into the sun to make it out.

"What is that?" I asked.

"I think...a star-horse carriage," Orin said, awe coloring

his words. "I've never even seen one. Star-horses are super rare."

"It's my father's personal carriage," Tristam said, and Orin placed a hand on my arm as my fists automatically started to rise. It wasn't my fault; I was like Pavlov's dog—needing to punch every time Tristam said something infuriatingly pretentious. Which was ALL. THE. TIME.

The carriage came to a halt before us, and I couldn't help my mouth falling open. The huge silver-gilded coach was pulled by four ebony stallions with coats that shimmered like the Milky Way on a dark night. They snorted and stamped their hooves, sending sprays of starlight off like sparks. They were mesmerizing—perhaps the most beautiful things I had ever seen.

I barely heard as Patricia announced the teams for the last leg and explained that we would be journeying under the sea to the land of the Mer Folk. I had the most powerful urge to vault onto the velvet back of one of those magical beasts and ride like the wind.

Orin tugged my hand as the rest of the contestants filed into the carriage. I let him tow me forward, shooting one last longing glance over my shoulder at the beautiful ethereal beasts. I guess I didn't come this far only to give up and ride off into the sunset.

The inside of the carriage was plush and opulent, gilded with silver and gold and upholstered with thick crushed velvet. Orin sat looking at the floor, his fingers digging into the bench beneath us as the carriage rose into the air, dipping and swooping like a swallow. I pressed my face to the window, wishing they would open so I could hang my head out like a dog. Faerwild sure was beautiful. Especially from afar, when it couldn't kill you.

The carriage banked, and I caught sight of the island city

of Elfame. I had been convinced Cass was there until I thought I saw her at the Sylph Court. But maybe that had been my imagination. She could still be in that city. I just needed to get there.

We circled the bay from the city and eventually touched down on a white sandy shore. We filed out and met our camera crews, who were outfitted with cameras in special waterproof covers. I gave Ben a little wave, and he gave me a thumbs up.

Patricia turned to us, dressed in a green and blue leaf dress like she was heading to a Hawaiian luau. "At the end of the Sorcery Trial, each team was given a gift from the Faerie King himself. These gifts will enable you to navigate the next leg of this Trial—the dark underwater world of the Mer Folk. This realm is even more dangerous than those lands you have tread before and has never been seen before on television. Be on your guard. Trust your teammates. And may the best racers win."

20

———

I exchanged a quizzical look with Orin. Were we just supposed to plunge into the water and swim? I guess I wouldn't mind that, the blue water lapped lazily against the pale sand, inviting me in. The sky overhead was clear, the sun shining upon us, warming my face.

I'd never been to the Caribbean, but I could imagine I was there. This, actually, wouldn't be a bad spot for a vacation. It was a pity that's not what we were here for.

It very quickly became apparent we were going to be transported to our destination by boat. Not a nice yacht. No, that would be too easy. Two long canoes, decorated with flowers and each with an oarsman, pulled up to the beach near us.

Sophia grabbed Tristam's hand and ran to the nearest one, eager to secure her seat at the front. It was fine by me. I'd rather be behind the pair of them anyway. That way, they wouldn't be able to stab me in the back on the way there. Tristam, ever the gentleman, took the front spot leaving a pouting Sophia to take the second seat.

I looked at Orin and shrugged. We were really going to have to do this. He took my hand the way Sophia had taken Tristam's, but when we were at the boat, he helped me into the third seat before taking the fourth and final place himself, our oarsman behind him. With a little shove from the FFR staff on the beach, both boats were off. I peeked a look at the other team. None of them seemed any happier that we were heading out into the open water, and Dulcina, at the front, looked positively green. Water was obviously not her element.

At least, seasickness was not something I had to worry about. Sophia lounged back in the small canoe and lifted her legs over the side, trailing them in the water. She posed herself like a supermodel in a perfume commercial, and I noticed all the camera crews in their motorized boat were filming her. Even Ben seemed to have his camera trained on her sultry profile, tilted to soak up the sun.

My mind was coming up with so many possibilities for what was about to come next that it was almost a relief when we got to our destination and docked against a small wooden platform of about ten square feet. The other team had been taken to an identical platform about a hundred yards from where we were.

The oarsman helped Orin out and then held his hand down to me. I was surprised to find that he wasn't human, but some strange aquatic faerie with luminescent blue scales covering his skin. I needed to pay better attention to my surroundings. Being stuck in my head was going to be no help during the next leg.

I stepped onto the platform beside Orin and waited for the other two to join us.

As soon as Tristam was on deck, the oarsman dropped a

shimmering clam on the boards next to him, jumped back into the boat, and began to row away. We were well and truly stuck with no land nearby. There was only one direction we could realistically go.

I peered into the murky depths, hoping to see something, but the sea was cloudy, and I couldn't make out anything.

I pulled out the small vial I'd been keeping safe since the Sorcery Trial. The two pearls inside looked so ordinary that I couldn't see how they would help us at all. Tristam picked up the clam and then pulled out a similar vial and passed one of the pearls to Sophia.

Theirs were different from the ones Orin and I had been given. Where ours were small and white and insignificant, theirs were larger with a beautiful pink sheen.

"I think we swallow these," Tristam announced, popping one into his mouth, followed quickly by Sophia.

Almost immediately, I saw the change in them. Sophia's face contorted into a look of anguished shock, and she fell to the platform, gasping for air, her teeth bared in pain. Her wetsuit split at the seams, and her beautiful legs grew scales, suctioning together until they formed a tail. Holy crap, Sophia was a mermaid.

The charge of magic dissipated, and Sophia pushed herself up to a seat, her face pale. Her shock seemed to drain away as she regarded her new tail, flipping it with a grin. She dangled her fins into the water and waved at the boat of camera people who lapped it up. "Mermaids are so on trend right now," she purred, before slipping majestically into the water and disappearing below the surface.

Tristam had followed suit and now sported a similar tail. He also gave a wave and dove head first into the dark water.

"After you," I said, popping the pearl in Orin's hand. He threw it back into his mouth and swallowed. I popped mine in my mouth, and as it traveled down my esophagus, I waited for my transformation. I didn't really want to be a mermaid, but I'd be damned if I let Sophia and Tristam show us up.

Pain snaked through my body, hot and sharp, seizing my lungs. I looked down at my legs, but my body remained the same at it always was. "What's happening?" I croaked in horror as my throat began to close.

"Quick, get into the water." Orin placed a firm hand on my back, pushing me into the sea. I made a huge splash with my belly flop. It was hardly the graceful dive Sophia had completed, and I was sure the cameras had caught that too. But, oh, sweet relief. I could breathe again. I expanded my lungs, and water flooded my mouth, causing me to choke. I could breathe underwater, but barely. The effort just to keep oxygen flowing was immense.

Anger flooded through me. Why had Tristam and Sophia turned into merfolk while Orin and I looked like a couple of flounders out of water? At least, it was calm under the surface, and I could see slightly better. I floated, enjoying the serenity that only being underwater could bring.

"Cheating rat bastard," Orin cut through my moment of peace. His voice was strong but distorted under the water. We were both in our human form. No pretty mermaid tails for us.

"I should have known when I saw the pearls," he continued. "Did you see them?"

I nodded. They were hard to miss. "Tristam managed to screw us over before we even started."

I thought back to the person who'd given me the pearls. It hadn't been Tristam, and the ones Orin and I had swallowed had been in my possession the whole time. "Actually I don't think it was Tristam," I began.

Orin looked at me, incredulously. His dark hair floated about his head like a wavy halo. "Please tell me that you aren't sticking up for that pretty boy? Not after everything that he's done to us."

I shook my head, keen to dispel that particular thought. "It was the king who gave me the pearls. They looked that way right from the start. They were never large and pink like Tristam and Sophia's."

Orin's eyes widened even further, giving him the appearance of a startled guppy. "You think the king is trying to sabotage us?"

I thought back to Zee and Genevieve's rings that didn't work in the first leg of the race and the refusal to give me a replacement. If anything happened to me, I was a goner.

"Maybe. It wouldn't be the first time."

I was about to say more, but a large splash told me that we were no longer alone. Ben waved at us from a little underwater submersible that just enveloped his body.

Below us, Tristam and Sophia were already swimming into the smoky depths. They glided with grace, swishing their tails in unison until they were nearly out of sight.

"We'd better catch up, or we'll lose them," I said, gurgling each word.

But it was clear that it wasn't going to be easy. Without tails, we couldn't cut through the water the way the others did, and every stroke was an effort, as I had to concentrate on breathing as well as swimming.

Orin was having no better time of it than I was, and when I looked over to him, I saw his lips were turning blue.

"This isn't worth it," I said, my words creating bubbles that lazily floated to the surface. If we weren't careful, we were going to die down here. I didn't want to be out of the race, but there was no way the FFR bosses would let us continue, impaired the way we were. I tapped Orin on the shoulder and pointed upwards.

When I crested the surface, my breathing went from a struggle to completely impossible. A pull on my leg had me going right back underwater.

"Those pearls have closed your natural airway," Orin said. "We're stuck down here until the magic wears off."

"How long will that be?" I asked, trying not to panic at the thought of it. I didn't have many fears, but drowning above the water certainly qualified.

Orin shrugged. "Just stay as calm as you can. If you panic, you'll use more oxygen." He pulled me into a hug and held me tightly until my near panic attack subsided. This was the closest we'd ever been to each other since our almost kiss the night before, and this time, our skintight clothes made it feel like we were both naked. I closed my eyes as Orin's strong pectorals pressed against my chest, and his arms wrapped around me, sheltering me from whatever horrors lay ahead.

My body's reaction to Orin's closeness was undeniable. My pulse quickened, my breathing became deeper, and the desire to touch him under his wetsuit became unbearable. I could have stayed like this forever, locked together, a tangle of limbs, pretending we weren't in the middle of a stupid race. A stupid race that was rigged by the one hosting it.

I took a deep breath...or a deep pull of oxygenated water, and this time, my senses cleared. Being this close to Orin had done the trick. When I opened my eyes, I saw Ben filming everything. I couldn't bring myself to care. Whatever was going on in the outside world would have to wait. We'd need all of our focus here to make it through this leg.

"Come on," I said, pulling back from Orin. "We should catch up with the other two."

He seemed reluctant to let me go but nodded.

We inverted our bodies and plunged into the darkness.

21

My muscles burned, and my body was completely numb by the time we reached Tristam and Sophia, who hovered near the sandy bottom. They were giggling and frolicking, flipping their fins about. I wished I had a trident to fork them with.

"What took you so long?" Tristam asked.

I glowered at him. "Our pearls were a bit different than yours."

Tristam nodded. "That's right. The pearls were given out by order of how we finished the Sorcery Trial."

I frowned. "What do you mean?" I vaguely did remember the king mentioning something like that.

"It was a reward for finishing further ahead. The first team got the most powerful pearls. You guys finished last, so…" Tristam trailed off. Roger that. Worst pearls.

"Great," Orin said, throwing up his hands. "So they stack the deck in favor of the winners."

"Don't hate the player, hate the game," Sophia said, watching how a lock of her hair floated before her in the water.

I narrowed my eyes at her. I hated the player and the game. Though, I'm not sure that had the same ring to it.

"You guys aren't going to slow us down, are you?" Sophia asked. "Because we'll leave you."

"You can't," I said. "We all need to finish together. Now let's stop yapping and open the damn clam." Tristam was still holding the clam that the oarsman had dropped on the deck. I'm sure it was the clue to where we were headed next. The end of the Elemental Trial. If we made it. My teeth were chattering, and my head felt faint from the dark and cold.

Tristam and Sophia set to prying it open, and Orin approached me. "Come here, I want to try something." I let myself float near him as he closed his eyes. He was doing some sort of magic.

I felt the most delicious warmth cocoon me, and I audibly sighed in relief. "Ohmygawd, that's amazing."

But he wasn't done. I felt a tingling in my eyes and then it was like a little shield slid down over them, protecting them from the briny salt water. I could see more clearly through the murk, too, like I had a searchlight.

Orin opened his eyes. "Okay, try to kick your feet."

I did as commanded and shot upwards. "Woah!" I hollered, backpedaling with my hands, which also seemed supercharged.

"It's good? It worked?" Orin asked.

"I feel about a thousand times better," I said, breathing a sigh of relief. It was still strange down here, but I didn't feel like I was going to die of hypothermia anymore.

"Okay, great, I'll do the same to myself." He closed his eyes again, performing the enchantments on himself. God bless that faerie's magic.

"Got it!" Tristam exclaimed.

I shot to his side to inspect the pearlescent interior of the clam. It held a tiny, intricate model of a city.

"It's Elfame," Tristam said. "Just across the bay."

Sophia and I looked at each other, and for once, I think we had the same thought. "What's the catch?" she asked.

"There's an entire merfolk city between here and Elfame," Orin answered, his jaw set in a hard line.

"So?" I asked. "Let's get going."

"The merfolk are not...friendly," Tristam said. "They are intensely territorial, and just a step above savages. My father sent my brother once to renew a basic treaty, and he ended up a prisoner for a week."

That was the first time Tristam had ever mentioned his brother. From the stony look on his face, he didn't like to.

"So, we go around," Sophia suggested.

Tristam shook his head. "They control the entire waterway. We'd have to circle around much of the city to avoid them. It would add days to our journey."

"And this is a race," Orin said. "We need to go through."

"It'll be fine," I offered, my words sounding unconvincing, even to myself. "We'll just stay low, stick to the shadows. Go incognito."

"Incognito with two bright blinking personal submersibles following?"

We all turned to look at Ben and the other cameraperson's submersibles, floating a few yards away. Crap.

"Anyone have any other ideas?" I asked.

Silence. Tristam shook his head, running a hand through his golden locks. His face was pale, and I didn't think it was just the cool water. "We'll have to go through. But we stay close together. Move quietly. Don't touch anything. And if we run into them, don't act cocky. Don't try to fight. There will always be more of them lurking, and they'll stab first, ask questions later."

I swallowed a mouthful of salt water. This was the first time in the race I'd seen Tristam anything but annoyingly self-assured. And surprisingly, I didn't like it one bit.

IT WASN'T SO BAD, really, once Orin had ocean-ified me. We swam in silence, skimming the bottom of the sea, navigating around protruding coral and tall seaweed fluttering in the currents. Fish darted by to inspect us—brightly-colored minnows and silver schools moving in unison. We passed purple starfish and an orange-spotted sea eel and even a translucent jellyfish glowing purple that Orin assured me was not poisonous. Like the surface of Faerwild, the depths of its sea was filled with beauty and wonder. And, I was certain, danger.

A skeletal hulk of wood caught my eye off to the left, and I found myself examining it. It was a faerie shipwreck. I didn't know how old the poor vessel was, or how long it had been there, but something about it tugged at me. At the magic within me. I started swimming past, but the pull grew stronger—more insistent. I turned about, biting my lip. We'd been swimming for hours, and nothing bad had happened. Time to make some interesting TV before the producers sent a water dragon after us. Or something. I didn't even know if water dragons existed.

"Look," I nudged Orin. "I'm going to check it out."

"Jacq, Tristam said we should stick together," Orin protested, but I was already swimming towards it. A quick peek couldn't hurt. Just enough to satisfy whatever strange intuitive hit I seemed to be getting.

Orin caught up to me as I reached the wreck, peering through the gaping hole in the side. "I can't believe I just said that. Don't go in there Jacq—" Orin said, but I darted inside before he could finish his sentence.

Inside the wreck was spooky, the low light of the sun barely filtering into this place. I could make out the remnants of the inside of the ship, wooden tables rotting, ropes covered in green algae, a brass bell overturned and coated with barnacles. This wreck must have been here a long time.

"Jacq, get back here." I heard Orin shout at me, his voice warbly in the depths.

"Just a minute!" I called. Something glinted in the corner, underneath a pile of broken dishes. I felt the tug again. It was definitely pulling me that way. I swam closer, peering at the wooden floorboards, carefully moving one of the plates.

A crab exploded sideways from beneath the plate, and I screeched, startled by its flight.

"What?" Orin burst through the hole into the wreck, looking around for the danger.

I laughed, the release feeling good. "It was a crab. It startled me. That's all. I'm fine."

"Tristam and Sophia are going to get too far ahead. We could lose them," Orin said. He was clearly feeling antsy to get out of here.

"Now, you're dying to get back to your BFF Tristam?" I turned back to the corner where I'd seen the glint of metal. It was a pile of silver coins, six in all. They looked ancient. "Look!" I said, holding up one. It seemed to pulse with energy in my hand. Maybe it was some sort of magic coin.

"I don't know what a BFF is, but this place is creepy as

hell. I feel like something is going to jump out to eat us at any moment."

I picked up the coins and slid them into a thin zippered pouch sewn into the hip of my wetsuit. Nice of them to give us pockets. As soon as they were safely on my person, I felt a sense of relief wash over me. Like I was supposed to find these.

"You're being paranoid," I said. "Nothing is going to jump out and eat us."

But as I moved to swim back to the window, my eyes caught another glinting light in the corner of the watery wreck. This one I recognized as the glint of teeth. And I realized how very, very wrong I'd been.

22

"Ohmygod," I said, the words bubbling out of my mouth.

Orin turned and let out an expletive that was lost to the deep. "Go!" he cried, grabbing my arm.

He didn't need to tell me twice. The two of us kicked off the bottom of the ship to propel us outside just as the shark torpedoed towards us with its rows of wicked teeth bared, ready for its next delicious meal. Human—followed by a faerie dessert.

We burst through a ragged hole in what used to be the deck of the ship as the shark slammed into the wreckage where we'd just been floating. Even with Orin's spell on our arms and legs, the shark was fast. There was no way in a million years we'd outpace a shark with only our legs to push us along. Maybe with Tristam and Sophia's tails, but we didn't have those...

My panicked mind was rebelling over the idea of being shark lunch, but luckily Orin wasn't going to give up without a fight. He pointed his hand towards the shark, and a beam of light shot out, stunning the beast as it tore through the rotting deck after us. But it wouldn't be stunned long, and now that we were out in the open sea, we had nowhere to hide. I pumped my arms and legs furiously, but the effort to move at a quick pace was excruciating. My lungs burned, and my heart pounded with the pressure of the getaway.

In the distance, I saw Tristam and Sophia swimming lazily ahead. So much for sticking together. They hadn't even noticed our absence. Okay, I could argue that I was the one that took a detour, but what kind of teammates were they if they hadn't even noticed?

"Tristam," I screamed in the vain hope that he'd be able to help, but it was no use. We were too far away, and my voice didn't travel very far underwater.

"Forget him," Orin panted, taking my hand and pulling me forward in the current.

I risked a glance over my shoulder, and I could see he was wrong. Someone needed to come to our aid and if not Sophia and Tristam, then who? I glanced around in a panic, hoping Ben was nearby. It was officially against the rules for him to help us, but he knew I didn't have my ring to save me anymore and he wouldn't let me be eaten by a shark. Then I saw him. He was up ahead in the distance, filming Sophia along with the other cameraman. He was supposed to be with us at all times! If I survived this, I was going to have strong words with him about priorities. Keyword: *if*.

I dug deep and swam with every last bit of energy I had. My muscles screamed with effort, but we needed to catch up with the others. I wasn't sure how that would help—it would probably only mean that the shark was going to have a four-course meal instead of two, but I needed a goal to keep myself moving.

I kept my eyes on the twin lights of Ben and the other

cameraman's submersibles, focusing my energy on them like a lighthouse in a storm. I was surprised at how rapidly they were getting brighter. In fact, my panic-addled brain couldn't quite register the fact that Tristam and Sophia had turned and were swimming hurriedly toward us. Had they actually seen us fleeing from the shark and were coming to help us? It was out of character for sure, but they did need us to pass the finish line with them whether they liked it or not.

It was only when they were close enough for me to see the terrified looks on their faces that it dawned on me that I was wrong after all. Neither of them had enough empathy to care if Orin and I died and yet the pair of them looked as petrified as I felt.

And then I saw why. It had nothing to do with the giant shark chasing Orin and me. They were being chased too...by a dozen merfolk wielding golden tridents.

We kind of crashed together in a watery tangle of arms and legs and fins—Tristam and Sophia hastily backing up, Ben and the other cameraperson on each side of us. Time seemed to stand still as we gaped at each other in shock. Unfortunately, no one had given the shark the memo, because while the rest of us had come to a complete stand-still, he was still coming for us. I turned and screamed as he opened his jaws wide, ready to bite.

A flash of light hit him square in the mouth and instead of chowing down on cowgirl a la wetsuit, the shark clamped his jaws shut just an inch from me, thrashing in pain. The hulking beast turned its tiny eye towards us, mean mugging us before it flicked its powerful tail swam and away.

"You saved us," I cried, turning to the merfolk. My body was trembling, and I felt sick to my stomach, but I was alive...and grateful. "Thank you so much!"

My gratitude was rewarded with the butt of a trident to my stomach. "You dare to taunt a shark, an honored denizen of the deep, inside my own territory?" the nearest creature demanded. The mermaid was nothing like any I'd seen on TV or in print. She was fiercely beautiful, with long, flowing, black hair, but there was a savagery about her, from her sharp teeth to her strange angular face to the green color of her skin. There was no cute seashell bra or singing side-kicks. These mermaids and mermen were all completely naked, just as all the other creatures of the deep were. The FFR editors were going to have to do some interesting blurring before this scene was fit for prime time audiences.

"Well?" the mermaid asked, prodding me sharply with her trident. If it wasn't for the strong material of my wetsuit, I was sure she would have pierced the skin.

"I didn't taunt it. It followed me. It wanted to eat us."

This was clearly not the answer the mermaid wanted to hear. She issued a command in a language I didn't understand, and immediately, ten other merfolk came forward and grabbed hold of Orin, Tristam, and Sophia.

They tried to grab the cameramen too, but they couldn't get purchase on their submersibles. Ben and his camera-mate turned and revved their engines, roaring out of reach. I thought the Faerie king had promised that the camera crews would have safe passage throughout the race, but perhaps he didn't hold as much control down here as he thought.

The only one not being held was me, but as I had a trident pressing down on my belly, I was hardly in any better a position. Could one reason with an angry mer-chick? I had to try. "We only want to pass through your city if we may. We mean you no harm."

The mermaid threw her head back and laughed, and the others followed suit. It was an eerie sound, a dozen merfolk laughing. It was like an accordion being played underwater with thousands of tiny bubbles rising to the surface.

"You mean us no harm?" The mermaid echoed my words back to me. "Causing us harm shouldn't be your biggest worry. I have an army of merfolk awaiting my command. You should be more concerned about the harm we can do to you."

"Don't say anything else," Tristam warned me. Not that I was planning to. What more was there to say?

The mermaid grimaced at him then turned her attention back to me. "You will come with us." I guessed I had no choice in the matter.

She turned me around, and the crowd of merfolk parted, letting us through. Getting kidnapped by merfolk wasn't on my to do list when I started the day, but if they hadn't been around, I would have been ripped to shreds by shark teeth. So I suppose I couldn't complain too much. I swam slowly, even with a trident held to my back. After racing from the shark, I didn't have the energy go any faster. The mermaid made no complaints about my speed, however.

We swam in silence for about fifteen minutes before the strangest sight caught my eye—an underwater city beyond anything I could have imagined. It was nothing like the legend of Atlantis. There were no marble statues and crumbling buildings. This place looked...almost modern. The neat rows of buildings, some so tall that they would soar above us, was a strange contrast to the wildness of the merfolk. So was all the color. The buildings were decorated with shimmering mother of pearl mosaics and reflected every shade of pink and purple. Brightly-colored fish swam in and out through the open windows and doorways. And inside, the buildings glowed with bright faerie lights in deep blues and aquamarine. It was beautiful.

"What are you going to do with us?" I asked when we finally stopped at the edge of the city. This close to it, I could finally see why much of it looked pink. Many of the buildings were made of coral.

I turned to the mermaid to see what she had to say. She wasn't planning to kill us. If she wanted us dead, she could have left us for the shark. I had convinced myself this logic was sound, which was the only reason I wasn't totally freaking out right now.

"That's not up to me to decide. My father will pass judgment."

I really didn't want to know the answer to the question, but I asked anyway. "Who is your father?"

She puffed her chest out with pride. Somewhere a mile or so back, Ben's eyes were bugging out of his head—at least, they would be if he was filming this. Where was he? "My father is the great king of the Merfolk."

Great! Another freaking spoiled faerie royal brat! A princess to go with our prince!

THE MER KING'S audience chamber was the size of a college football stadium...if the interior of said stadium was built like a conch shell. The tall ceilings were ribbed with mother of pearl inlay coating and the curving walls held seats of a sort, where merfolk floated now, watching us with baleful gazes.

The princess poked me with her trident as I slowed, not wanting to face whatever was coming. But when I caught sight of the raised dais with the elaborate coral throne, I couldn't help but forget my own problems for a moment. Because four other prisoners knelt before the throne—four prisoners I recognized. Dulcina, Phillip, Ario, and Molly. I guess our team wasn't the only one who hadn't been unable to slip through the Mer kingdom unnoticed.

The Mer king rose to his full height at the sight of us, his huge arms open wide. "My daughter returns with the other interlopers," he boomed out, his deep voice scratchy and raw.

I tossed a black look towards the princess. She had made it sound like I had offended them by being chased by the shark, but it turned out that they knew we were here and had come searching for us. At least, it wasn't my fault we'd been caught.

The king looked nothing like the jovial, possibly-senile King Triton from *The Little Mermaid*, one of my and Cass's favorite movies as kids. No, he looked like a formidable Poseidon, his long dark hair undulating in the current, his muscular chest and arms covered in gold and silver armor. When he smiled, he bared a row of razor-sharp teeth that reminded me uncomfortably of the shark I'd just met. His crown was encrusted with pearls and other jewels, perhaps stolen from some shipwreck like the one Orin and I had explored.

The merfolk escorting us poked the back of our knees and we fell to the ground next to the other contestants. I experienced a brief moment of satisfaction at seeing Ario and Molly look so out of their element. *Just try to seduce someone now, playboy*, I wanted to croon at the incubus. Between their fingers stretched webbed flesh like that of a frog. It must have been the effect of their pearls. Dulcina and Phillip had mer-tails, like Sophia and Tristam did. They must have been tied for first or something after the Sorcery Trial.

I took in all these details to avoid taking in the rest,

which included the bristling weapons and teeth of the hordes of strange creatures surrounding us. Suddenly I had a painful longing for the sylph palace—for the downy lemon meringue pie I'd eaten after dancing with Orin. What I wouldn't give for a riddle about poo right about now.

The silence of the throne room was starting to become oppressive when Tristam finally spoke, addressing the king. "I am Tristam Obanstone, crown prince of Faerwild. We are here on a sanctioned mission jointly operated by the humans and the fae. We mean you and your people no harm. We are only passing through. But I must respectfully insist that you release us."

The king chuckled; the sound, like grinding gears, was not comforting. "You must insist?" he asked. "Land dwellers have no claim to insist upon anything within these waters. Beneath the sea, you have no jurisdiction, crown prince. This is not Faerwild. This is Deephold. And I am king here."

Tristam blanched. "Of course. I did not mean to suggest that you do not have full authority here. But I know that you and my father have a diplomatic relationship. It was my understanding that our passage through, for purposes of the race, was discussed, and even agreed to."

The king had negotiated our passage through the Mer territory? That was interesting. Though I suppose it would have been incredibly irresponsible of the FFR to send us into dangerous territory without making some sort of prior agreement. Which is exactly why I had assumed that's how it went down.

Tristam continued. "I would ask that you allow me and my companions to continue on our way. We travel to Elfame. Perhaps you could grant us passage, in the interest of furthering fae-mer relations."

"And if I have no interest in furthering fae-mer relations?" the king asked. "As of late, your people have been abusing these waters. Perhaps what I truly desire is war."

The Merfolk around us cried out at that, cheering and howling and drumming their tridents on the stones of the floor.

I looked around nervously. This was derailing quickly, even for the FFR.

"Surely there must be something we can offer you in exchange for our release," Tristam said. I thought of what he had said earlier. That his brother had been held hostage here. They had been able to negotiate his release somehow.

The king boomed, drawing up to his full height. The guy was built like the Rock. "You deign to think that you have anything to offer me, King of Deephold, Lord of the Seven Seas, Defender of the Tides, most honored of all Aquatic Life?"

"Well—" Tristam began, but the king had clearly heard enough.

"You will take them to the Abyss." The king waved his hand to dismiss us. "I will consult with my advisor about what should be done with them." I exchanged a worried glance with Orin. The Abyss? That sounded...unpleasant.

The princess pulled me to my feet, as did the other contestants' captors. We swam out of the building, the shouts and jeers of the onlooking merfolk following in our wake. I really didn't think I liked mermaids anymore.

The Abyss turned out to be just about what it sounded like. We took a tunnel that led us deep below the Mer city, the darkness oppressive around us. My pulse skittered in my veins the farther we got from civilization. This felt like the kind of place you took someone to execute them and then drop them in a mass grave. I could barely see in the low light of the tunnel; without Orin's enchantment over my eyes, I would have been totally blind.

Just when I thought I might scream to release the tension, the tunnel started to ascend, and we came out into an area lit by the dim light of what appeared to be glowing algae. We floated in a narrow chasm—I couldn't even see the light of the surface above—and below us was nothing but the black depths.

"The Abyss is where we keep our most dangerous citizens," the princess said, nodding for us to move forward. I saw now that there were openings in the sides of the cliff, strung with thick bars embedded into the stone. They were jail cells.

We neared one of the cells, and the merfolk herded us all into it. It wasn't exactly roomy, but there was enough space that we weren't all piled on top of each other. But when the door closed and one of the mermen turned the key in the lock, it felt like it shrunk by half.

"How long are you going to leave us here?" Dulcina asked, floating up to the bars, peering out at the retreating forms of the merfolk.

"That's up to my father," the princess said with a toothy grin. "If I were you, I'd pray to whatever surface god you worship that he doesn't just leave you to the fishes."

23

———

I f I thought being in a race with this bunch was difficult, being locked with them in a cell under the water was ten times worse.

Gazing through the bars, I could see nothing but dim light and the occasional fish that ventured down this deep. The weight of the water was oppressive, and I felt as though I was being squeezed from all sides, giving me a headache and making my mind cloudy. It wasn't helping that I could hear anguished screams coming from a nearby cell. I didn't think it was helping anyone else either, because the panic I was feeling seemed mirrored on every face in the cell.

Dulcina had retreated to the back of the cell where she'd pulled her tail up to her chest and was quietly rocking, her eyes closed. Small murmurs came out of her mouth that sounded a little like a nursery rhyme, and even in the dark light, I could see she was shaking.

Molly was sulking, her arms crossed and a grimace on her face like she'd just been grounded by her parents, and Tristam was holding onto the bars, his knuckles white with barely concealed rage. Only Ario, Phillip, and Sophia kept their cool. Ario smirked when I glanced his way as if this was all some kind of joke, and Sophia ignored us all and kept herself busy by running her fingers through her hair like a comb. Phillip swam around the small cell, checking the walls and the bars for something—Cracks maybe? A secret button that opened the doors? Who knew?

I was somewhere in the middle of the panic scale, but at least I had Orin by my side. He was close enough to let me know he was with me, but not close enough to cause discussion. The last thing I needed was everyone speculating about the pair of us. From way above, a searchlight shined down. I squinted, and as it approached, I recognized it as Ben's submersible. Excitement ran through me. I'd never been so happy to see a cameraperson in my life—especially Ben. He'd do everything in his power to get us out of here.

"Jailbreak," Ario said calmly, when he too spotted the submersible, causing both Molly and Sophia to stand. Only Dulcina stayed in her wrapped up position on the cell floor. I think she was way too terrified to even notice there was someone else with us.

"Ben!" I exclaimed. "The Mer king locked us up. Can you get us out?"

Tristam pressed his whole body to the bars. "Talk to my father. This is unacceptable."

Ben pretty much ignored Tristam's tantrum and looked at me instead, his eyes troubled through the glass of the submersible. Even before he spoke, I knew it wasn't going to be good news.

His voice sounded tinny through the speaker. "We've been looking for you all over. The FFR was made aware that you'd been taken by the Mer king. King Obanstone has already spoken to him."

"So when are we getting out?" Tristam asked, visibly

relieved. Having a king for a father certainly came with benefits, and this time it seemed, it would benefit us all.

"You aren't. The Mer king made it clear that your father has no jurisdiction down here. He only let the camera crew in because he wanted to show the world that no one is above him and he can do what he pleases in his own kingdom. He's aware of who you all are and your level of fame. I think he planned this all along—it's why he originally agreed to allow you passage. Your father is doing what he can to try to secure your release, but he doesn't know if he'll be able to."

Tristam slammed his hands into the bars at the news. I guess he wasn't used to his father not being able to get him out of scrapes.

"Can you fix some rope to these bars and pull them with your submarine thingy?" Molly asked hopefully, but Ben shook his head.

"Not unless I want to end up in there with you. There are hundreds of mer-people up there. There's no way I'd manage to get you out without being seen. Look, I gotta go."

"Are you fucking kidding me?" Tristam shouted, directing all his anger at Ben. "You came down here to tell us that there's nothing that can be done? Is this funny to you?"

Ben directed a steely gaze at Tristam and held his hand over what looked like a microphone to muffle it. "This isn't my doing. You got yourself into this mess. I only came down here to tell you that your father is doing what he can. I also came down here to film you because that is my job, so congratulations, you were caught on camera looking like the giant prick we all know you are."

Normally I'd have cheered; it was about time someone stood up to Tristam. But I was angry too. How could the FFR have gotten us into this mess? They sent a reality show into a war zone! I gave Ben a half-hearted wave as he turned around and left us, once again, to the darkness.

As Ben's light dimmed and disappeared, I felt the darkness and weight wrap around me like an old friend. That was it then. There was no chance of escape, and the king couldn't save us.

But hey, at least, we were all famous!

I thought of my parents back home. Soon enough they'd be watching this, along with half the world. I turned my thoughts to the FFR. John would be going apeshit at this turn of events. It would make amazing TV, the tension of all of us captured and locked up. The will they/won't they escape or get released. It would be great for a week or so, but after that...who would watch? No one, that's who. The eight of us would be down here for god knows how long and the viewing public would find something else to watch. It wouldn't be long until we were a distant memory with no one left to save us. It was a depressing thought, but it was a million times better than the next thought that invaded my mind.

"How long does the magic of those pearls last?" I asked. I hadn't worried about it before—I'd thought we'd be in and out of the underwater kingdom within a few days. But it was clear we were way off script here.

A panicked look shot around the people in the room as it dawned on them what I was saying. Most enchantments didn't last forever, and I couldn't imagine the FFR had given us pearls that would make us permanent underwater denizens. Which meant that at some point, the magic would be up, we'd all turn back to our normal selves, and seeing that none of us were water-based faeries, every single one of us would drown.

"Can we use magic to get out?" Orin asked. "Melt the bars or something?"

"I tested the entirety of the cell," Phillip said. "It's thick with counter-enchantments. I think any attempts to compromise the bars will alert our captors if it works at all." Oh, so I guess that was what he'd been doing.

"I'm going to use my ring," Molly said, but Ario jetted across the room and grabbed her hand to stop her.

Orin gave me a look as the pair wrestled, looking down at his own ring, our only hope of getting out of here. I knew what he was thinking. Zee and Gen's rings hadn't worked. The FFR or the king had let them die. Even if the race staff could get in here to rescue us, would Orin's ring work?

I'd never heard Ario raise his voice before, but now it echoed around the cell. "Don't. We've come too far. I'm not letting you give up on my behalf. We've only been in the cell ten minutes. We might find a way out."

"What if we don't?" Molly cried defiantly.

I had to give her credit; she was strong and feisty and was putting up a good fight against Ario who was almost twice her size. I wouldn't want to fight him for sure.

"There's no point anyway," I said quietly. Both Ario and Molly turned to look at me. "The FFR can't get us out; King Obanstone can't get us out. Not down here. Even if you all use your rings, it won't change that fact."

Molly broke into tears as she realized it was the truth. Her ring was nothing but a decoration on her finger.

This was it. I gnawed on my lip and thought about the magic pearls. How long would they last? Orin's and mine were the least powerful, so it stood to reason that we'd be the first to die. To drown in an underwater cell, the most famous people on the entire planet. I turned to Orin and slipped my arms around his waist, pressing myself into his chest. I didn't care anymore what the others thought. I needed him. We were all going to die anyway, so what did it matter about the gossip?

Orin spoke whispers of comfort in my ear and wrapped his arms around me. I snuggled my face into his shoulder while he smoothed my hair down. There were probably worse ways to die. I wasn't looking forward to having water gushing into my lungs, but wrapped up in Orin, I could, at least, pretend that wasn't going to happen...for a while.

"Let's think. Is there another way?" Phillip asked. "Can we bribe them somehow? There must be something they want."

Tristam sighed. "They're obsessed with precious gems and metals. You saw how much bling the king had on. They especially love ancient things—relics of the deep. But I don't have a treasure trove hidden in this wetsuit, do any of you?"

A ringing noise sounded as a guard ran the end of his trident along the bars, making me jump.

Immediately, Tristam was on him, throwing himself against the bars. The guard had ventured too close to the cell, and Tristam managed to grab him by his neck and pull him right to the bars. "Let us out of here, or I'll squeeze the life out of you."

I'd never seen Tristam look so angry. It was terrifying. The normally cool and calm facade had dropped completely, leaving nothing behind but the monster he was. I raced towards him and kicked his leg. "Stop!"

The guard's face was already beginning to turn blue under Tristam's grip.

Tristam glared at me, his teeth bared.

I started to shy back but then held my ground. "The guard can't help us if you kill him first!"

My words seemed to sink in because Tristam let go of the guard, who swam back clutching his throat.

"Please, sir," I shouted to him once his color had returned to normal. "What can we do to get out of here? There must be something we can give you?"

Tristam slammed past me, almost knocking me over as he swam to the back of the cell. "Yeah, ask him to let us out as a favor. That'll work better than my way!"

Sophia, who'd been quiet until now, swam up next to me and fluttered her eyelashes at the male. When she spoke, her voice was different, sultry. "We'll do anything," she purred. "And I mean anything..." She ran her hand down her body in a way that made me gulp.

Ario, not to be outdone, came forward and tried his sexy mind trick on the guard and repeated Sophia's words, gripping the bars strategically to display his rippling muscles. Just in case the guard was into men instead of women, I guess. Behind me, I heard Orin chuckle. At least he was finding humor in the situation. "Let's all have a mer-orgy!" he whispered in my ear, and it took everything I had not to let a bubble of deranged laughter escape. I didn't even know how mermaids had sex. I mean, with the tails.

But it didn't matter. The guard's face darkened, as if the thought of fraternizing with a faerie of the land, let alone a human, disgusted him. I was surprised at his restraint, to be honest. I couldn't imagine many people would turn down the twin charms of Sophia and Ario, but he just hovered there, shaking his head at both of them.

I wondered what I could offer him. Certainly not what the seduction twins were. If he didn't want Sophia, there was no chance he'd want me, but I did have something she didn't. Tristam had said that they valued precious metals and ancient things. Perhaps...I fished about in my pocket and pulled out the coins I'd found earlier. Something had drawn me to them—it had felt like my magic had called out to them. Maybe this was why. They were so small and insignificant, I had no clue if they would be enough, but I held one up to him. "Would this be of interest to you?"

The guard's eyes widened. Finally, we'd found something he could lust over. He swam forward to grab the coin from my hand, but I pulled it back. "Where did you get that?" he rumbled.

"An ancient shipwreck. There were more where those came from. An entire chest full of treasure. You get us out of here, and I'll give you these coins and tell you where to find the rest." I figured it wouldn't hurt to oversell things a bit.

"I can't get you out of here. It's impossible," the guard croaked. There were shadowed bruises forming on his neck where Tristam's fingers had gripped.

"There must be a way out. I can see you have keys to the cell. How about opening the door and we'll find our own way from there?" I nodded in what I hoped was an encouraging manner.

He thought for a moment. To sweeten him up. I passed one of the silver coins to him, keeping five back.

"You'll never escape," he said, but his hand drifted to a pouch around his waist and pulled out the keys. "The whole of Deephold knows you are here, and none of them have any interest in letting you go."

He put the key in the lock, and I held my breath, wanting to scream from the suspense. *Turn the key!* We were so close... "The second you reach the top of this ravine, a hundred merfolk will pounce on you, and you'll only end up back in here...or worse."

He turned the blessed key. *Hallelujah!* The second the

lock clicked, Phillip pushed on the barred door. It opened outwards, almost knocking the guard over.

"What if we don't go to the surface, but swim through the ravine?" I asked as the others barrelled out of the cell behind me.

The guard only shrugged his shoulders. "No one swims the ravine. It's not called the Abyss for nothing. You'll only die if you try. But that's your choice."

"We'll take our chances."

24

I gave him sketchy directions to the shipwreck where I'd found the coins and hurried after the others. Orin had hung back, waiting for me.

The Abyss was black as the night sky, but without any of the comfort of stars. Sporadically, a glowing fish swam by, or we passed a piece of algae that throbbed faintly with light. I hated this place. If I never went in an ocean again, it would be too soon. Strictly a land girl for me, from now on. At least, we'd gotten out of that cell, though.

"Do we know where we're going?" Molly asked in a hushed voice. It was strange, the eight of us being allies. Nothing like the threat of a slow, agonizing death in a deep-water prison to bring people together.

"If I recall my history," Tristam said, "the Abyss is near the neutral zone. This trench runs perpendicular to it, away from Deephold proper. If we stick to the trench, we should have only a short shot in open water to make it to safety, once we come up."

"Seems like they only need a short shot to kill us,"

Sophia mumbled, but when Tristam shot her a look, she forced a smile. "We'll be fine."

"What's the neutral zone?" I asked. "Is that where we'll meet Captain Kirk?" I said with a chuckle.

No one laughed, and Phillip just rolled his eyes. No *Star Trek* fans? I pursed my lips. Tough crowd. "You really know nothing about faeries, do you."

"Enlighten me, genius," I shot back.

Phillip shook his head. "The neutral zone is territory between the Mer kingdom and the upper realm of Faerwild —it's a shallow stretch of water. Both kingdoms are supposed to keep their soldiers out of it—that way there are no accidental skirmishes. Misunderstandings."

"If we make it there, we should be home free," Tristam added.

"Sounds like as good a plan as any," Orin admitted. Well, he was downright agreeable. The jailbreak must have put him in a good mood.

"Everyone circle up for a moment," Ario said, and we pressed closer together. The fact that no one protested showed how much this leg had freaked us all the hell out. Ario closed his eyes, and I felt the tightness of faerie quora magic settle upon me. It made me want to scratch.

"What'd you do?" Sophia asked.

"It's a spell to keep us incognito. I didn't like what that guard said. If we're going to be passing through, I thought we should do so without notice."

"An invisibility spell?" I asked hopefully. "Will it keep the merfolk from seeing us?"

Ario shook his head. "The invisibility magic I know involves refracting light. It won't work down here. But I doubt whatever is prowling down here uses its eyesight. This should keep us from...smelling good."

We all nodded. Okay.

We swam on in silence, the cold water pressing down around us. We kind of drifted into our pairs, swimming through the channel two by two. Tristam and Sophia were swimming in front.

Ever since I had realized the pearls might wear off, my lungs had felt tight and strained. I shook off the feeling. I was just being paranoid, psyching myself out. They wouldn't have sent us down here with spells that would fail mid-leg. But, perhaps we'd already been down here longer than the FFR producers had anticipated. I pressed a hand to my chest, feeling a panic attack coming on.

I felt someone take my other hand, and turned to see Orin. He squeezed. "I've got you. It's going to be okay."

And I felt better, for a moment. But then I saw a flicker of movement in the corner of my eye. Against the dark wall, something moved.

I squeezed Orin's hand in a stranglehold, pointing frantically. Ario, Molly, Dulcina, and Phillip saw my frantic motion, and slowed, shying against the other rock wall of the trench. But Tristam and Sophia still swam on before us, clueless.

I held my breath as the rock wall just...came away before my very eyes. Because what I was looking at wasn't rock. It was just camouflaged as that. It was a massive eel, the size of a tour bus. Its eyes were tiny black orbs, little help down here in the gloom. But it had other senses. And it was big enough to swallow us in one gulp.

The eel slipped through the water like a silent assassin, following after Tristam and Sophia, who were chatting in low tones. Its bulk passed within inches of me, and I squeezed my eyes closed, struggling to stay calm. To stay still. I forced my eyes open as it passed, its tail fluttering the little motes in the water before us.

Maybe it couldn't see them or smell them, but it could sure as hell hear them.

Dulcina and I exchanged a panicked glance as the eel neared Tristam and Sophia. A moment of indecision warred in me. They were both jerks who had cheated and schemed their way to the front of the pack. But they didn't deserve to die, did they?

Orin clamped his hand down on my mouth, and I struggled against him, elbowing him in the stomach. He let out a stream of bubbles, doubling over and releasing me. Freeing me to scream, "Look out!"

The eel spun around with shocking speed, abandoning its prey and heading straight toward us. Crap. Orin and I darted down low, swimming with all our strength. The eel crashed into the wall above us with concussive force, sending a shower of coral and kelp over us.

I cringed at the power of the attack but kept swimming, heading back toward the direction of Elfame, and hopefully, safety. Not that the eel would know to respect the neutral zone.

I looked over my shoulder and saw that the eel had spun and was heading towards us again. The thing could sure as hell hear my frantic paddling and bubbling breath. It was getting closer, and I could see its mouth opening, the blackness inside total and complete.

"Hey!" Tristam shouted from ahead of us. The eel flicked his head toward the noise.

"We all need to stay still!" Ario shouted, from a ways back. Easy for him to say, he didn't have a giant disgusting eel hovering two feet from him. "If it can't see or hear us, it will go away."

But it was as good a plan as any. We weren't going to be able to outrun the thing. Orin grabbed my hand, and we pressed into a little alcove of rock. The space just barely fit both of our bodies, and I had to twist my neck awkwardly to fit my head in. From here, I couldn't see the others, just the bulk of the body of the eel as it floated, seeming to decide what move to make next.

It apparently decided to return to the location where it had left its most recent potential snack. In other words, us. It undulated in the water, turning its muscled body so it floated down, so its head was even with our hiding place. It turned its beady eye towards us, and then its snout, swirling the water around us with its sniffing.

Orin and I were tangled together in a knot of stiffened limbs, desperate with fright. Ever so slowly, I saw him raise one hand. He was preparing to cast a spell. I shook my head ever so slightly, catching his eye. If he cast a spell, the creature would know we were here. And we had nowhere to run.

The eel's nose butted against the rock above us, testing. I squeezed my eyes closed, waiting for it to bump into me and realize I felt different from the other rock, that I was spongy and edible. My pulse roared in my ears, taking over all my senses. I would never get to find Cass, to unravel the secret of her note. I would never hug my mom and dad again, or eat barbecue from Wild Willie's, our favorite spot. I would never go for another run along Santa Monica Boulevard, stopping to watch as the sun slipped below the horizon. I would never get to kiss Orin. Damn it, why hadn't I kissed Orin?

I felt a little shake, and I peeled one eye open. Orin put his mouth next to my ear and whispered, "It's gone." The warm bubbles of his words tickled my ear as relief flooded me like a warm tide. I was so overcome with elation that I took his face in my hands and pressed my mouth to his. Orin's lips were cold, his body stiff with surprise, but the contact filled me with heat, warming me to my core.

Realizing what I had done, I pushed against Orin, but he caught me around my shoulders, pulling me back toward him and kissing me again. This time, there was no surprise, and his arms surrounded me, his body molding into mine. His lips and tongue moved in a sensation so delicious that almost getting eaten by a giant eel suddenly seemed totally worth it. If it led to this.

I heard a throat clear behind us, and we broke off our kiss. Phillip and Dulcina were floating a few feet away. "All clear," Phillip murmured, before flipping his tail and swimming to join the others.

Dulcina gave us a shaky smile and followed.

I pressed my lips together to keep from grinning, turning back to Orin. He hadn't managed to keep the smile away. It lit up his face, transforming it into something even more achingly beautiful than usual. "We better get going," he said quietly.

"Yep," I added, threading my fingers through his.

We continued through the deep, and gradually, the sea floor came up to meet us. We were clearly getting to the end of the abyss. I felt like I was floating along on the buoyed current of my and Orin's kiss. I kept wanting to glance over at him, but I didn't. Instead, I kept replaying it in my mind, the way the energy seemed to curl through me when we touched, the expert way his tongue flicked itself against mine...

"Jacq, Orin," Tristam said as he and Sophia settled into pace beside us.

Orin and I kicked forward to join Tristam and Sophia. Tristam lowered his voice. "We're nearing the end of the

Abyss. When we get into the neutral zone, it will be game on. We need to make a break for it to finish this leg first."

I looked at him in disbelief. He still cared about the stupid race?

"Agreed," Orin said, nodding with determination. I turned my shocked look to him. We'd all almost died back there. How could anyone really think about finishing first?

"I can see the top of the cliffs," Tristam said. He was right. The color of the water was lightening around us, the temperature warming. The end of the cliffs that made up the abyss trench was visible above us. "Let's get below the others, and when I signal, we swim for it with everything we've got, okay?"

Orin nodded, and I huffed but gave a curt nod. We'd have a talk about priorities later.

The four of us made our stealthy move, swimming below Phillip, Dulcina, Ario, and Molly, who were ascending towards the surface.

Tristam held out his hand. He raised one finger...two... but he never got to three. For a golden trident streaked through the water before him, narrowly missing his head.

"The merfolk!" Sophia cried. A horde of mermen and women were swimming towards us, shouting battle cries. It seemed our escape was not entirely unnoticed.

25

"**S**wim!" Tristam screamed as though we weren't already doing just that. Now that the water had cleared, I could see the ocean around me, and I didn't like what I saw. Directly in front of us, the sandy ocean floor rose, but as far as I could tell, it still had a long way to go until it breached the surface.

About two hundred feet ahead, I could just barely make out a shimmering magical wall that stood imposingly before us, spanning from the sea-floor to the surface. This must be the border between the Deephold and Faerwild—the neutral zone. If we made it that far, we'd be home free.

Hightailing it toward us from the opposite direction of the merfolk was an FFR submersible. One of our camera crew. Great, they could get the great FFR Mer-slaughter on camera.

Tristam and Sophia were breaking away ahead of us, swimming powerfully for the shore. The four above us were swimming as fast as they could, but the merfolk were so close to them that their capture seemed inevitable. I could only watch helplessly from below as the muscled bodies of the merfolk blocked out the light. There were just so many of them.

My lungs started burning something fierce, straining for air. Was it panic at the attack? But no, I was overcome with certainty that the magic of the pearl was failing. I looked at Orin, and he was pressing a hand to his chest, his dark eyes wild. His pearl was failing too. I had a powerful impulse to swim for the surface, but with a hundred merfolk above us, getting the hell out of Deephold had to be my top priority.

Ario, Molly, Dulcina, and Phillip launched an all-out magical assault on the merfolk. Ario shot a bolt of purple magic at the mass of them, but either the merfolk were clever enough to deflect it, or there were just too many of them. Phillip cast some spell that seemed to suck the water out from around some of the merfolk, which left them gasping for air. But one of the creatures must have cast a counter-spell because within seconds the liquid rushed back around them. The other contestants needed help!

But Orin kept a firm grip on my hand, kicking towards the shore, staying low to the ground below the melee. "The Merfolk are concentrating on the other teams. If we help, they'll do the math and realize there are two more."

I understood what he was telling me, but still, I could hardly face leaving them in the middle of a fight. *Coward*, my mind whispered. But as my lungs burned, my instinct of self-preservation won out, and I kicked forward. We didn't have much time left.

My lungs screamed for relief as Orin pulled me through the depths, keeping as low to the ocean floor as possible. As it was, only a couple of the merfolk had even noticed us, focussed as they were on Molly, Dulcina, Phillip, and Ario. Because I couldn't tear my eyes away, I kept finding myself tangled in weeds and choking back sand and grit, but it was better than the alternative.

I could only watch in horror as the events unfolded.

The Merfolk howled in anger at the magical attack, and one of the Mer-women jabbed her spear into Ario's gut. I was shocked by the violence of it, by the blood tinting the sea red around Ario's doubled over form. It seemed that what started as a mission to capture was quickly turning into a slaughter.

Orin gripped my hand harder as Dulcina, the slowest of the four, was caught by the wrist, a merman spinning her around violently. He grabbed her other wrist, pinning her hands together. She thrashed in his grasp, but he was too strong. Was he going to stab her next?

Tristam and Sophia were close to the shimmering wall now, and Orin was intent upon pulling me through the water as my whole body had completely given up and was starving for oxygen. Ario was floating with closed eyes, and Molly and Phillip were fighting for their lives. Ben's sub was closer, but he couldn't interfere—which left me. And what could I do? I didn't know magic. But then on seeing Tristam's retreating form, a spark of memory hit me. I had done magic a few times before. Sitting on the roof of Hennington House, for one.

I tugged on Orin's hand to slow myself. "Don't say it," Orin said, turning and reading the expression on my face.

"Dulcina's in trouble! We can't leave her!"

Orin shook his head. "The magic from the pearls is running out. Neither of us can breathe underwater now even if we wanted to. They're going to have to figure it out themselves."

But I couldn't leave, even though the pain in my lungs was unbearable and my vision was starting to swim. My senses felt hazy, my limbs sluggish. "Just give me a second." Pulling all my energy into myself I concentrated it into a single spot in the very core of my being, then with as much strength as I had left, I shot the energy out towards the merman that held Dulcina's wrist.

Unlike Orin and Ario's magic that shot out of them like bolts of lightning, there was nothing to see with my pathetic attempt beyond a slight displacement of water. I couldn't be sure if it was my doing or a swift kick from Dulcina with her tail, but the merman holding her lost his grasp and spiraled away. Dulcina, now free, flipped in the water, pulled off her ring and pushed the button.

A beam of light shot into the air, breaking the surface of the water. It only took a few seconds for a team of FFR faeries to come plunging into the water like Navy SEALs, shooting stunning spells at the merfolk.

It was strange—how the frantic movement of the battle transformed in an instant to peaceful floating forms, as if they were frozen in time. In the corner of my eye, I saw the submersible approach us, saw Ben's chubby cheeks through the glass windows. He was filming the rescue, but when he turned to look at me, I saw him mouth the word "Jacq!" Which was strange, because everything was getting dark. Why? I wondered. Had the sun gone behind a cloud? I realized, too late, what it was. Here, on the sea floor, 100 feet from safety, I'd run out of oxygen. I was going to drown.

The last glimpse I had was Orin's stricken face, his dark hair floating in the water.

I FELT a sharp pain to my cheek and the distant sound of Orin screaming my name. All of a sudden, my lungs expanded, and beautiful, wonderful oxygen filled them. My senses cleared, and my eyes fluttered open.

Ben's face filled my vision, his blonde curls a halo around him in the water. Ben? What was Ben doing here?

There was someone pressing their hand over my face, and I struggled against them, but iron hands held me still. I looked around in a panic before I finally realized what it was. Ben and Orin were holding me still while Ben pressed a portable breathing mask attached to a little oxygen tank to my mouth.

My vision finally cleared, and I nodded. Ben pointed at me and then motioned to take a deep breath before he pointed at Orin and himself. I nodded again, understanding. They needed the mask too.

I took a deep breath and Ben took the mask away, giving it to Orin. Orin breathed deeply, and Ben kicked to the side, to where his submersible was floating, the glass top open, its cockpit flooded with water. Hopefully, the thing wasn't totally fried. It didn't look like it was designed to be opened underwater. Ben had gotten out to save me. I wondered briefly if it meant we had forfeited the race. But I quickly realized I didn't care. This race had gone sideways days ago. It wasn't worth dying over. Cass wouldn't ask that of me.

"Hold on to the sub," Ben said silently as Orin passed him back the facemask. My lungs were beginning to burn again but Ben had been holding out longer, so I couldn't complain. Orin, Ben and I all situated ourselves along one side of the sub, holding onto the edge of the open cockpit. Ben reached in and pushed a button and the engine started chugging, towing us slowly towards shore, and safety.

Ben handed me back the mask, and I took the opportunity to look up. The FFR staff were completing their rescue, I couldn't see Ario, Molly, or Dulcina anymore, and I could just glimpse Phillip and one of the faeries being pulled towards the surface, a harness rigged between them. I wondered if the others had made it out safely. I wondered if Ario was alive. The guy was a complete dick, but he didn't deserve to die as a mermaid shish-kabob.

In the water around them, a hundred angry frozen merfolk floated, howling and screaming their anger and discontent. I wouldn't want to be anywhere near them when that stunning spell wore off. Which, from the flicking of one mermaid's tail, it was starting to.

I passed the mask back to Orin. "Can this thing go any faster?" I asked Ben, pointing at the mass of merfolk.

He nodded and reached into the cockpit to turn a knob. The sub roared to life, and the three of us held on tight as it shot towards the shimmering barrier that designated the neutral zone. Safety. We were going to make it.

A trident clanged off the side of the submersible, startling me so much I almost lost my grip. I looked back and saw that a few of the merfolk had broken free of the spell, and were in pursuit. A red-headed male was in the front, his huge chest and neck covered in tattoos. His jagged teeth were bared, and his eyes spelled murder. He held a four-pronged trident with wicked barbs and was hefting it like a javelin.

A shiver went through me as we passed through the magical barrier. Behind us, the merfolk were coming up short, not willing to breach the border. We had made it. We were safe! I let out a sob of relief, struggling not to take in water. Happy tears mingled with the salt of the sea.

Ben reached in and turned down the speed, hitting another dial that started taking us up towards the surface. Towards blessed air.

With my one hand still attached to the sub, I gave Orin

an awkward hug, burying my face in his neck. We'd made it. Then I turned to Ben to give him a hug, but froze as he stiffened, his face a mask of shock.

"What—" I started to ask, but my words fell away as red tinged the water around us. And I saw the four barbs protruding from Ben's chest.

26

———

"**B**en!" I screamed, grabbing his shirt as he released the side of the submersible. We were rapidly ascending now, and the sub burst through the surface of the water, pulling us up with it. I gasped for air as I tried to take in what had happened and my shaky hands fluttered around Ben's pierced body. He had taken a trident in the back; the wicked barbs had pierced all the way through his body.

Blood bubbled from his mouth as he tried to speak.

"Stay still," I said, my shock so powerful it felt like a physical thing. We had made it. We were safe. Ben wasn't supposed to get hurt. The camera crews were off-limits...

"We need to get him to shore," Orin said.

"There's no time!" I screamed. "He's bleeding out!" I grabbed Orin's hand and wrenched his ring off his finger and pressed the button before he could object. Nothing happened.

"Arghhh," I screamed, the ragged sound ripping from my throat. I threw the ring into the sea with all my might. Fucking cheating sabotaging faerie bastards!

"Jacq! Hold him." Orin lunged into the cockpit of the submersible, his front half hanging over into it. He surveyed the knobs and buttons and turned one, and the craft started chugging for shore.

I cradled Ben's body with my one arm, the other numb hand clinging to the side of the craft. "It's okay Ben, we're going to get you help," I said.

He was looking at me with his kind eyes, his lips tinged blue. "Jacq—" he said.

"You were so brave," I said, tears streaming down my face. "You saved my life. If you hadn't gotten me that oxygen, I would have died. I'm not going to let anything happen to you. You're going to be fine, okay? There are magical doctors here, and they'll fix you right up."

"—can't feel...my legs," Ben said. His face was so pale.

"That's totally normal," I said, searching for whatever line of bullshit might bring him comfort right now. "The blood is coagulating around the wound, to stop the bleeding."

He let out a rasping laugh before he mouthed one word. "Liar."

I felt my feet touch the soft sand of the bottom, and I let go of the submersible, focusing on cradling Ben's body. The long handle of the trident was still jutting out of his back, and I didn't want it to hit the ground and rip his wounds further. "Help me," I gasped.

Orin slogged through the chest-deep water and came around to Ben's other side. "Keep him on his side," Orin said, and we hauled Ben's limp body through the crashing surf, onto the beach.

The scene before us was incongruous. The graceful spires of Elfame stretched up before us, glittering in the brilliant morning sun. In the sprawling streets below, green trees and vines softened the pale stone walls of homes and beachside restaurants. The white sand beach was filled with chattering faeries and FFR staff—I spotted Patricia in a tight white dress interviewing a bedraggled Sophia and Tristam. It was like everything was normal—but everything had changed.

"Help us!" I screamed as Orin and I lowered Ben onto his side, collapsing into the sand beside him. "We need a doctor!" I knelt down and wiped Ben's curly hair off his forehead. His eyes were closed, his face white as the grave. *No, no, no.* "Don't you leave me, Ben," I sobbed at him. "You fight. You're a fighter. Don't let this place win."

A human and a faerie in FFR blue and silver ran across the beach, falling down beside us. "Step back, please," the human woman said, "let us work."

The faerie male, silver-haired and silver-eyed with long canines, took Orin's place at Ben's back, and Orin came around, pulling me to my feet, wrapping his arms around me. I leaned into him, soaking up his strength, but I couldn't take my eyes off Ben. Off his still form. The crimson blood leaking into the soft sand. The glint of the barbs of the trident protruding out where Ben's generous heart should be.

"You can save him, right?" I asked. "Get him into surgery? Or—a spell? You can save him!"

The human was holding her finger to Ben's neck, feeling his pulse. She shook her head at the other one. "You?" she asked.

The faerie male passed his hands over Ben's form, closing his eyes for a moment. Hope blossomed in me. Was he doing a healing spell? But then he opened his eyes and shook his head too. He stood, brushing sand off his knees. Without his support, Ben's body rolled to the side, propped up like a macabre puppet by the staff of the trident. "I'm sorry. He's gone."

"Save him!" I screamed, throwing myself at the faerie. Orin caught me around the waist, trying to corral my flailing arms. I felt like I was coming unmoored from myself, this place, this person. The only thing that mattered was saving Ben. He hadn't deserved to die. Whatever the rest of us had done or planned or schemed to be here, Ben had been innocent. They had promised to protect him.

"Even magic can't cure death," the faerie said gently. "His wounds were too severe. If we'd gotten to him the moment he was injured maybe...but as it was, the barbs pierced several of his major organs, including his heart and his lungs. I'm sorry about your friend."

"But we pressed the button! To summon you!" I screamed. "And it didn't work!"

"That doesn't make sense," the human doctor exchanged a confused glance with her companion. "The rings should bring instantaneous aid."

"Jacq, come on," Orin said, trying to calm me. But I didn't want to be calm. Was I the only one who saw how fucked up this was? They had sabotaged us, just like they had done to Gen and Zee! They were dead, and now, so was Ben!

Patricia and the producers were approaching, Tristam and Sophia at their side. The cameras were gathering too. Did they have no decency? Filming this poor boy's death for ratings? I turned to Patricia, savage in my fury. "You promised to keep him safe! And then you threw us in there, to a kingdom you had no control over, with pearls that didn't even work, and rings that were supposed to save us but weren't even worth the cheap metal they were made of! You did this! The king did this! They sabotaged us!"

Patricia went pale, and Tristam stepped forward. "What are you talking about?" he asked.

"Jacq, calm down," Orin locked his arms around me, and I struggled against him, wanting nothing more than to slap the fake sorrow off Patricia's perfect face. She knew exactly what I was talking about! "Don't say something you're going to regret," Orin hissed in my ear. Even quieter—"Don't jeopardize Cass." My sister's name cut through the haze of my fury and grief, bringing me back to myself ever so slightly. We thought the sabotage of Gen and Zee's ring had something to do with the Brotherhood and whatever work Cass was trying to do. If I accused Patricia publicly, I could clue in the bad guys, whoever the hell they were. Fury bubbled in me. This sucked. The world should know what they had done! But I couldn't do something that might hurt my sister...

I lowered my voice, my words coming out strong and fierce. "This disgusts me. You—disgust me." I pointed at Patricia, at the producers. "Ben's death is on you. All of you. For putting money and power over human life. I hope Ben's family sues the shit out of this show, and I hope they win." With that, my tirade was over. The anger drained from me like water down a drain, leaving nothing but emptiness and aching sorrow. I fell to my knees besides Ben's body and wept.

27

―――――

For a full hour, they tried to convince me to leave Ben's side, to head to the palace where the ceremony would begin. Eventually, it was Orin that managed to convince me to go with him, wrapping me in an oversized FFR hoodie. I barely remembered the carriage ride back to the palace where we'd all stood in front of a huge crowd not one week earlier.

"I can't..." I sobbed onto Orin's shoulder. I didn't finish the sentence. I didn't need to. Orin knew exactly what I was talking about.

"You don't have to do anything. I won't let them make you." His warm arms around me and his soothing tones were the only thing that stopped me from completely losing my shit. As it was, I was on a knife's edge. The FFR staff were at least wise enough to give us our own carriage. If Patricia or Tristam or anyone else, for that matter, had even tried setting foot in here, there would have been carnage. My heart might have been raw, but I was pissed as hell too, and the tears I shed for Ben were red hot. This was supposed to be a TV show, but it had ended up as a free-for-all where death was becoming commonplace, and no one seemed to care as long as the ratings were high.

In the human world, this whole thing would have been shut down weeks ago. Zee and Genevieve's death would have put an end to the Fantastic Faerie Race. Fantastic my ass! But of course, we weren't on Earth, and we were still lining the pockets of some obnoxious fat cats in Hollywood. When I got home...if I got home, the first thing I was going to do was tell John where he could stick his job. I'd seen what show biz was like and I didn't like it one bit. I needed to get home. Home to my parent's ranch in Montana. I needed to be somewhere where things made sense, and people actually gave a damn about each other. Somewhere where I was needed. Loved.

It occurred to me that I was already feeling those things, bunched up as I was in Orin's arms. He needed me. He hadn't told me he loved me, but there was definitely love in every movement he made. The way he held me close to him, the way he stroked my hair, the way he wiped my tears away. If it wasn't for the horrendous weight crushing my chest, I'd probably have never been happier. It was a strange thought, the emotions whirling within me, They were at completely opposite ends of the spectrum, but I felt them both keenly.

The carriage slowed down, and Orin's protective grip on me tightened.

When we came to a standstill, and the door opened, thousands of flashes lit up the interior of the carriage. What the ever-loving fuck was happening now?

"What's that?" I croaked, thinking the worst—fireworks, bombs. My oxygen-deprived mind couldn't process what was happening.

"Photographers," Orin hissed in my ear, picking me up.

It was just as well that he did. I didn't have the energy to walk.

"Get out of our way!" I'd never heard Orin sound so angry, and he'd had his moments. I nestled my head into the crook of his neck and squeezed my eyes shut as he carried me through the media. I couldn't see them, but I could hear them all jostling for position, trying to get a better view. I knew what this would look like on TV and I hated it, but at the same time, I didn't care. I just wanted to be on my own...well not quite on my own. I wanted to be with Orin. The noise died away as Orin took us further from the crowds, but a voice stopped him. A voice I recognized.

"You need to go to the ceremony," the Faerie king said. "You can't come in here until you do what you signed up for."

My blood boiled. "Signed up for?" I said, dropping out of Orin's embrace and facing the king. "I signed up for a TV show, a bit of entertainment for bored housewives to watch on an evening. What I didn't sign up for was a bloodbath. I didn't sign up for watching my friend die. I didn't sign up for any of this shit." A guard nearby stepped forward, unsheathing his sword, but the king waved him back.

"Nevertheless, you have to talk to the crowds. The people are here to see you. Whether you want to do it or not is not really my concern, but the price of my hospitality is for you to comply with your obligations. If you don't want to play the game by my rules, I'll gladly have my servants escort you to a portal back to the human world right now, but you'll never be allowed in again while I'm in charge."

I balled my fists, trying to keep a hold of my temper. The urge to punch him as I had punched his son was overwhelming, but I knew if I did, the guard would come at me again, and this time, he wouldn't stop.

As much as I didn't want to go on stage and talk to Patricia in front of thousands of people, I wanted to leave Faerwild less. Cass was still here. Giving up meant giving up on Cass.

Orin pulled me to the side out of earshot of the king. "He's bluffing. I heard them talking on the beach. Dulcina used her ring, and Ario was badly injured and resigned from the race. They need us if they want there to be a third trial. That's why they're going to overlook the fact that we broke the rules."

Oh, right. The rule that said your cameraperson couldn't help you. The rule that would have kept Ben safe if they'd given us stronger pearls, or if they'd given Orin a ring that worked, or if they'd not sent us into a lawless underwater kingdom with a score to settle against the land dwellers.

"But I'm not going to make you do this," Orin whispered. "Not the ceremony, not the next trial. I know how much you want to go home."

His words cut through the haze. He was giving me his blessing to give up the race? Even though my quitting would mean he'd lose his chance at freeing his parents from slavery. I couldn't ask that of him, could I? With a shock, I realized that it wouldn't just be Cass I'd be giving up if I quit now. I'd be giving up Orin too. If I could never come back to Faerwild, we'd be apart forever. As I looked up into his dark eyes, I could see the fear in them. He didn't want me to go, and yet he wasn't going to stop me if I wanted to. Some of my grief softened into something warmer, yielding. Love. I'd lost so much, I wasn't going to lose Orin, too. Even if it meant playing the game a little longer. I gripped his hand and turned my head to the king. "I'll go on the stage."

"Now there's a good girl," the king flashed a saccharine smile that made me want to scream.

With Orin's fingers interlocked in mine, we walked to the stage, escorted by the king's guard in case we changed our minds again. The second we stepped out in front of the people, a roar of excitement and cheering nearly burst my eardrums. This was definitely fame. So many people coveted it. Well, they could have it. It wasn't for me.

Patricia, with her usual smarmy, too-much-lipstick smile, walked over to us and shook both our hands. I let her because, hey, we were in front of a live audience. That and the rows of guards upon guards standing just out of eyeshot of the crowd.

Behind Patricia on a couple of colorful sofas, sat Tristam and Sophia, both looking as gorgeous as ever. How the hell had they had time to both change their clothes and get their hair and make-up done? Orin and I were still in our wetsuits, and though my hair had dried a while ago, it clung together in sandy and salty rattails around my ears.

"Welcome, Jacq and Orin. Come, sit down." Patricia patted the spare sofa, pretending as though she wasn't a hunter ready to pounce on her prey. "Let's all have a look at the highlights of the last leg, shall we?"

The large screens behind us flickered on and the story of the past week of our lives was recapped for the thousands of faeries in the crowd and millions of people back home. I sat cringing the whole time, wondering if they'd play back the kiss. That kiss I'd shared with Orin was my anchor, the only thing that was getting me through this, but it had been private. It wasn't for them, and I didn't want to share it. Thankfully, the kiss wasn't shown. Nothing in the Abyss was shown because no camera crew had gone down there beyond the time Ben filmed us in the jail. I noticed they cut the bit where Tristam was acting like an ass to Ben. Of course, they did. They wouldn't want to show their golden boy in a bad light.

Then they showed the dance in the Sylph Palace.

It was strange watching Orin and I dancing together—like watching a romantic movie where the two characters finally realize they were made for each other in the last scene. Except this wasn't the last scene. We still had another trial to go, and I wasn't sure if Orin and I would get our happy ending. Part of me wanted to keep our feelings secret, as we hadn't even talked yet about what we were, what the kiss had meant to us. But watching us on screen, there was no hiding it. The chemistry between us was electric. We danced like there was no one else on earth, just the two of us. Then I saw her. Cass.

I froze as on-screen me moved in to kiss Orin and then saw Cass. It *had* been her in the Sylph palace. The cameras had caught her perfectly. I'd thought it was the altitude playing tricks on my mind, Dulcina had said as much. But she'd been wrong.

Cass had really been there. And I had seen her.

28

My heart pounded in my chest, and my mind whirred as I took in what I'd just seen.

Patricia, unaware of my inner turmoil, started asking me questions about a romance between Orin and me.

But I couldn't speak. The shock of what I'd just seen filled my mind, making it impossible to process what Patricia was asking me.

"Jacq!" Orin shook my knee, bringing me back to the present.

"So," Patricia said. "You two look cozy. I think we can safely say you are more than just friends, right?"

She held the microphone to my mouth, as we'd been thrust onto the stage without a chance to get mic'ed up.

I wanted to scream, to tell everyone that it was none of their effing business, but doing that would win me no fans. Now that I knew I was right about Cass, I couldn't run the risk of being thrown out of Faerwild. "Orin and I have grown close in our time together," I said carefully. May as well give Patricia and the crowd what they wanted.

Across from me, both Tristam and Sophia pouted now that they were no longer the center of attention.

"You've watched us on TV, but out of respect for Orin, I'd like to keep our relationship private." It was as close to *none of your damn business* as I could get away with.

Patricia, knowing that she was going to get no more out of me, turned her attention to Orin.

"And you, Orin. What do you think of Jacqueline?"

"Jacq is the bravest woman I've ever known." He'd said that about me before, but now I knew he wasn't just talking about my ability to climb mountains or fight wild beasts. It ran much deeper than that. We'd shared more together in the past few weeks that most people go through in a life-time, and because of that, our bond had grown deeper than I ever thought possible.

I reached out and took his hand, not caring that we were on TV or that thousands of people were in the crowd watching us. That little gesture sent the crowd wild, causing Sophia's face to drop even further. Being upstaged was probably the worst thing that could happen to her.

"And Jacq, what's next for you and Orin? You've got one more trial to go, and I happen to know it's even more dangerous than the first two. I've had a sneak peek, and it's not for the faint of heart. Are you going to use that bravery that Orin was talking about?" She was trying to get the crowd excited with talk of danger, and they were lapping it up. But if she thought she was going to scare me, she was wrong. I just didn't care anymore. They could bring a starving lion onto the stage and ask me to wrestle it, and I probably wouldn't bat an eyelid. They'd already done the worst thing they could to me. They'd taken my friend's life. Nothing trumped that. Let them starve us, trick us, torture us. I was ready for anything they threw at us because I was closer to Cass than I'd been in years, and I was determined to find her before crossing the finish line.

I rehearsed some line in my head about being ready for anything, but before I could speak, the stage was plunged into darkness. At first, it was just the lights pointing at us, but then, the lights illuminating the crowds went too, and finally the ones in the palace behind us, leaving nothing but darkness.

A panicked murmur ran through the crowd, but it wasn't until the first explosion that the screams began. My hand was already in Orin's when the lights went off, but I tightened my grip as people around us began to panic. As far as I could tell, the explosion came from a patch of grass behind the crowd. That area should have been free of people—I prayed there would be no more deaths today.

All around me, screams punctured the air as people ran from the flames licking up behind them. It didn't help that the night sky was heavy with clouds, rendering the place completely black except for the fire that the explosion had ignited behind the crowds. The flames had the effect of funnelling the crowd forward, and I could see in the dim light that people were pressing against the stage, some even jumping the barriers keeping us separated. It seemed just seconds before the stage was flooded with panicked people making a run for it. Someone knocked into me, pushing me into Orin. The same person grabbed my wrist and squeezed it before disappearing into the darkness.

"Come on," Orin said, and we made our way blindly to the back of the stage and then down some steps. My ragged breath was loud in my ears, my legs numb with cold and exhaustion. Orin was leading us to the palace behind the stage. It wasn't ideal and could be the next target, but our options were limited. Either stay on the stage and risk being crushed or take our chances. And I didn't have it in me to think of an alternate plan. It was all I could do to keep moving, to stay on my feet and not collapse in a puddle, waiting for whomever these attackers were to come and finish me off.

But then, almost as quickly as the lights went out, they came back on, revealing a scene of complete chaos.

Someone in an FFR uniform ran over to Orin and me, grabbing us and shepherding the pair of us through the crowd to the relative safety of the palace.

Minutes later, Tristam and Sophia joined us, followed by a very rattled-looking Patricia and some more FFR staff.

"Come with me." The king appeared, ushering us through the palace to a room furnished with matching brocade sofas. "Stay here. I've instructed my guards to do a sweep of the palace, and there will be a number of them posted outside the doors of this room." He waved his hand, and a pot of coffee and some cups with the royal crest appeared on the small table.

Orin poured a cup and handed it to me. Sophia sat on the sofa in tears as the FFR crew rallied around her and Tristam sulked at not being allowed out. Once again I was trapped somewhere I didn't want to be. Okay, there weren't goblins or merfolk trying to kill me, but this threat was even worse. This threat was invisible. If it was not for the genuine panic on the king's face, I might have thought this was his doing, or a stunt to bring the ratings up.

Orin tapped my arm and pointed to a quiet corner of the room. Making sure everyone was caught up in their own conversations, Orin lowered his voice and whispered to me.

"I don't think anyone was hurt, and I don't think anyone was meant to be."

I'd thought the same thing. The explosion was terrifying

at the time, rattling my already ragged nerves almost to the breaking point. But in retrospect, it didn't seem much more powerful than a particularly loud set of fireworks. From what I'd seen, it had gone off far enough away from the crowd enclosure not to hurt anyone. "So what do you think it was? A warning?"

Orin shook his head and checked the others again. Everyone was wrapped up in themselves, not paying attention to us. "I think it was a distraction."

It made sense, well...as much as anything made sense in this place. "A distraction from what?

"I don't know, but I'm sure we'll find out sooner rather than later. Whatever this is, I think it's bigger than the Fantastic Faerie Race. There is something going on, and I think we've found ourselves right in the middle of it."

I nodded. The sabotaged rings. The Brotherhood of the Rose and Thistle. The splitting of our worlds. Cass. Everything was connected somehow, but between fighting beasts and solving riddles and mourning the death of another friend, I was hardly in a position to connect the dots. My mind felt hopelessly muddled. I took a deep breath and told him what I'd seen on the screen just minutes before the lights went out.

"Cass was up there?" Orin seemed surprised, but then pulled me into a hug. I wasn't sure what it was for, but I welcomed it, leaning into his warmth. He smelled of salt and blood, reminding me of the ordeal we'd just been through. He was so quiet I could barely hear him over Sophia's loud sobs and Patricia's swearing about the lousy phone reception.

Finally, he spoke. "We aren't safe. Until we find out what's going on, we stick together like glue and trust no one. Tonight you sleep with me." A few hours ago, the suggestion would have had me alight with excitement and nerves, but now, I was just confused. Confused and tired. I leaned into his hug, and it became just that. A hug for the sake of hugging. We clung to each other, adrift in a sea of confusion. In Orin's arms was the only place I felt safe anymore.

The door opened, and we pulled apart. The king walked in, flanked by a couple of his men. "The palace is in lockdown for the night. You may as well get some rest. We'll convene in the morning where we will brief you on the final trial. I'll have some staff bring some food up for you." He turned to leave. That was it? That's all we were getting?

"Was anyone hurt?" I called across the room.

The way the king looked at me sent shivers down my spine. It was almost as if he didn't even think to check on everyone. Perhaps he hadn't. "Not as far as I'm aware. I'll have someone update you all in the morning."

He left the room, and this time, Tristam was allowed to leave with him.

So it seemed that we were stuck here whether we liked it or not. But for the moment, I supposed it didn't matter. I was tired. More tired than I'd ever felt in my life and though it had been so long since my last meal, I wasn't hungry. I just wanted to curl up in a warm bed and sleep. I wanted to curl up with Orin and pretend none of this was happening. Pretend that we were just a boy and a girl without a worry in the world.

I asked a member of the staff to show Orin and me to our rooms, not that we'd need more than one. The guard nodded his head and beckoned us forward. I followed him, putting my hands in the pockets of the hoodie Orin had given me on the beach. My fingers brushed something. A piece of cardstock... or thick paper. Whatever it was, it hadn't been there earlier, and I hadn't put anything in there.

My heart pounded as I remembered the person crashing into me on the stage, the same person who'd lightly squeezed my wrist.

All along the palace corridors, my mind whirred with what it could be, and when Orin tried to take my hand, I had to push him away. I couldn't chance the note or whatever it was falling from my pocket and being seen by a guard. I could tell he was hurt at my rejection, but it wasn't for long. The second we were shown to a room, I slammed the door in the guard's face, locking it behind me.

I whispered to Orin what had happened, and he nodded. Pulling me to the bed, he pulled back the covers, and the pair of us hid, shielding ourselves from any hidden cameras. He magicked up a light source, and only then, could I safely pull the note from my pocket.

My breath caught in my throat as I took in the delicate swirls of Cass's handwriting.

"Cass?" Orin whispered. I scooted closer to him so he could read the note. It was brief, but it said all it needed to. *Come to the Goddess of the Moon at midnight. Bring Orin. -Cass.*

I let the note fall to the bed, stunned. I'd found her...or she'd found me. For the first time in two years, I was finally going to see my sister.

The threat of the Fantastic Faerie Race's final trial loomed over us, but that was a threat for another day. For now, I'd done what I'd set out to do.

I'd found her. And this time, I wasn't going to lose her again.

You can now read the final book in The Faerie Race series,
The Doomsday Trial.
Read on for a sneak peek!

IF YOU ENJOYED THE ELEMENTAL TRIAL...

And now for a Sneak Peek of *The Doomsday Trial*, Book Three in *The Faerie Race* trilogy!

You can buy the whole series now
   The Sorcery Trial (Faerie Race book one)
   The Elemental Trial (Faerie Race book two)
   The Doomsday Trial (Faerie Race book three)

29

CHAPTER ONE

I thought I'd been ready for the Fantastic Faerie Race. I thought I'd been ready for whatever I'd find over the Hedge in Faerwild, for the tests and challenges, even a little not-so-friendly competition. But the last few weeks had shown me how horribly, naively wrong I had been.

The race competitors had been trained for physical strength, for intellect, even our magical capabilities had been honed. But no one had prepared me for the emotional toll this race would take.

No one had even asked me how I would cope if someone were to die. No one had asked me what I'd do if my sister suddenly reappeared out of nowhere...and not a single producer or staffer had asked how I'd cope emotionally with the ever-present threat of my own demise.

There'd been talk of how dangerous it would be. We'd been warned to watch our backs, but I'd thought it was just the studio trying to scare us to make great TV. I hadn't believed anyone would really get hurt in here, much less killed—and yet, I'd seen three people involved in this godforsaken race die in a matter of weeks.

I gazed up at the ornate ceiling of one of the Faerie king's palace guest suites, these thoughts refusing to leave, my sorrow shredding at my heart with vicious swipes.

Orin's warm arm snaked over me, pulling me closer to him. I yielded to him, snuggling closer. In what felt like a sea of desolation, he was my only life preserver. If it hadn't been for Orin, I'd have completely lost it.

The palace staff had assigned us both rooms, but I'd followed Orin to his and curled up in his arms, adrift in my misery. Neither of us had bothered to undress, both of us falling into bed in the wetsuit-like FFR outfits we'd been wearing since we'd started the final leg of the Elemental Trial. Orin had fallen asleep first, his deep rhythmic breathing keeping me company as I counted down the minutes to midnight.

I hadn't been able to sleep a wink, despite the exhaustion weighing me down like a stone. How could I? If Ben's senseless death wasn't enough to keep me awake, the thought that I was finally going to see my sister after two years of searching kept my eyelids firmly open.

I'd read Cass's note so many times in the half-light of the moon that I knew every curve of every letter, and yet, I held onto it, fearful if I let go, it would somehow magically disappear. Taking Cass with it.

Come to the Goddess of the Moon at midnight. Bring Orin. - Cass.

That was all it said.

Outside a bell chimed. I counted the chimes as I had at every hour since we'd collapsed on the bed. Eleven.

I didn't want to, but I shuffled out from beneath the safety and warmth of Orin's arm and headed to the en suite bathroom. I unzipped the oversized FFR hoodie Orin had put on me while we waited on the beach, shivering and numb. I didn't even know who it belonged to. As I dropped it to the floor, something fell out of one of the pockets. Picking it up, I saw it was a small black leather roll, tied with ribbon. I untied it and found that when the leather lay flat, it formed a black mask, the kind that would go over your eyes for a masquerade ball. And what was more—there were two of them, one laid neatly on top of the other.

I furrowed my brow, holding them up. Where had they come from? Did they belong to the prior owner of this hoodie, or had Cass slipped these in my pocket with the note? If so, why?

Too drained to solve the mystery now, I lay the masks on the counter and showered quickly, washing the salt and sand from my body. Then, wrapping a towel around me, I headed back into the bedroom. Orin was still asleep. He was so heart-wrenchingly beautiful with his dark hair falling over his eyes, yet his sleeping face was contorted with worry. I hardly had it in my heart to wake him, but he was finding no peace in his dreams, and there was no way I was going to leave the palace on my own. Besides, in her note, Cass had specifically asked me to bring him.

I nudged him lightly, and he stirred.

His black-as-night eyes fixated on mine, and I became acutely aware that I was wearing nothing more than a towel. Orin grabbed my hand and pulled me towards him, bringing me into a kiss that shattered me to my very core. It wasn't a kiss of passion but of hope, of safety, of comfort. And yet, the touch of his lips upon mine brought tears to my eyes which fell between us, wetting both of our cheeks.

"Don't tell me my kissing is that atrocious," Orin said, rubbing a thumb across my cheek to wipe away the tears.

"The worst." I smiled, running a hand through his silken

hair. I couldn't quite believe I got to touch him now, that this was allowed. "It's eleven."

Orin nodded. "I have an idea of how to get past the guards. You get dressed, while I have a quick shower and I'll fill you in." He walked over to the bathroom, and a few seconds later, the sound of rushing water hit my ears.

Padding over to the one wardrobe in the room, I opened it to find a couple of FFR outfits, both in Orin's size, a suit and a couple of pairs of jeans and t-shirts.

I guessed that if I'd have slept in my room, my wardrobe would have had clothes tailored to me. But I didn't want anyone catching me sneaking down the corridor and questioning my motives for being out so late, so I pulled out one of the t-shirts and a pair of jeans and slipped into them. The jeans hung off me, but I found a belt to hold them up. I wouldn't win any fashion awards, that was for sure, but it didn't matter what I wore. It only mattered that I was going to see Cass.

Sitting on the bed, I fidgeted while waiting for Orin. I couldn't keep still. The minutes were ticking down, and though Orin had assured me he knew exactly where the "Goddess of the Moon" was, we still had to get past the guards and plan or no plan, it would take time. Time I couldn't afford. When the bathroom door finally opened, I heaved a sigh of relief and stood, but no one came out.

"Orin?" I padded to the bathroom, sneaking a look inside, but it was empty. "Orin?" I whispered again, the fear beginning to creep up inside me. Had they managed to take Orin somehow? It was impossible. I'd been watching the bathroom door out of the corner of my eye the whole time.

"I'm here."

I jumped in shock at the voice in my ear and turned, throwing an elbow into something solid.

"Ow! You hit me." Orin materialized in front of me, clutching his stomach.

"Sorry," I said, shaking my head. What the hell had just happened? "You were right there, and I didn't see you. Why didn't I see you?"

Orin's eyes crinkled at the edges, and a mischievous grin spread across his face. "It was my fault. You didn't see me because I was wearing this." He held up one of the leather masks I'd abandoned in the bathroom earlier.

"You're a master of disguise," I countered, still not taking his point. What did a cheesy masquerade mask have to do with this?

"You don't get it, do you?" Orin held the mask up and put it back on his face. Within a second he'd vanished completely.

I stumbled back a step. "Holy shit. You're invisible."

He pulled the mask off, reappearing again. "I found them in the bathroom. There are two of them. I was planning to try to put the guards to sleep, but this is much better."

"They fell out of my pocket when I was getting undressed. They must have been with the letter from Cass," I said, growing excited. "She thought of everything! A way to help us get out of the palace, undetected!"

Now that the shock of elbowing an invisible Orin in the stomach wore off, and the surprise of the invisibility masks had subsided a little, I grew keenly aware that Orin was completely naked—save for a white fluffy towel wrapped around his waist. His bare chest was lean and chiseled, his abs rippling downward in a perfect V, his strong arms roped with muscle. He probably didn't even have to do sit-ups, damn faerie metabolism. His pale skin looked like marble on a statue, and I longed to reach out and touch it. But a wave of shyness hit me as I realized how quickly we'd been breaking through the walls between us. It was all a little overwhelming. "You better get dressed," I managed, clearing my scratchy throat.

The glint in Orin's eye suggested that he knew just what my line of thought had been, but he stayed blessedly quiet. He dressed quickly, dropping the towel to the floor as he pulled on his pants. I found myself wishing he was wearing the mask because watching him was almost unbearable. His body was achingly beautiful and I'd finally seen it in all its glory, albeit for half a second while he dressed.

I needed to get my mind out of the gutter and onto more important things—like getting out of the palace and meeting Cass. I looked at my watch. It was already half past eleven. Sucking in a deep breath, I threw my thoughts of Orin's naked body to one side and began to pull on my shoes.

We tied the masks onto our faces, and Orin vanished once more. It was strange, when I looked down I could see myself like normal. "Did it work?" I asked. I felt a ghostly hand fumble along my side, searching for my own.

"It worked." Clinging tightly to each other, we headed out of the bedroom door and into the palace.

30

CHAPTER TWO

The Faerie king's palace was a huge austere behemoth filled with long empty hallways. Orin's room had been sparsely furnished, but there had been a few cozy touches—a plush carpet, a pot holding a strange night-blooming plant.

The palace itself seemed empty, as if the Faerie king hadn't taken the time to furnish the cavernous spaces that he lorded over. This was the place where Tristam had grown up? A pang of sympathy shot through me, which I squashed ruthlessly. No doubt his gilded childhood had been filled with fancy balls and friends and foreign dignitaries. He didn't deserve me to feel sorry for him.

It was strange walking through the wide empty corridors as if we owned the place, not needing to sneak or hide. I held my breath and kept my footfalls soft as we padded past two guards in the purple and gold livery that I had come to recognize as belonging to the house of Obanstone and the realm of Faerwild. The king's symbol—a clenched gloved fist (subtle, that)—was emblazoned in gold gilt across the doors we passed and stained into the leaded glass of the windows. It seemed to be some of the only décor he'd seen to.

As we continued to walk, I started to realize that getting out unseen wasn't the hard part here. It was figuring how the hell to get out in the first place. The palace was a maze. We passed a few servants here and there hurrying quietly, or pairs of guards flanking doorways, but we couldn't exactly stop to ask any of them for directions. We could hardly even whisper to each other for fear of being overheard. So we threaded our fingers together and walked silently, hoping that the next turn would be the one that would lead us to freedom.

We turned down a long hallway that seemed promising —at the end of it stood two tall, broad wooden doors crossed with iron bars. A servant turned from a side hall directly in front of us—a lovely faerie female with jet-black hair and arching eyebrows.

Orin's grip on my hand tightened painfully, and he let out an audible gasp.

The faerie woman froze where she stood, looking around, her pointed ears trained for the origin of the sound.

What happened next was inexplicable. Orin pulled his mask off, revealing himself to the woman.

"What the hell—" I started, but my panicked whisper was cut off by one wavering word.

"Mother?"

Holy shit! This was Orin's mom?

The look on her face confirmed it. Her dark eyes went from shock to delight to motherly worry in the span of an instant. "Orin," she cried. She looked around surreptitiously before hurrying towards us and grabbing Orin's arm, pulling him back into the side hallway she'd come from. "What are you doing out of your room?" she asked.

"That's all you have to say to me?" he asked, hurt playing across his handsome features.

"Of course not," she said, pulling him into a tight embrace and burying her face into his chest.

He wrapped his arms around her, and I looked away, feeling as if I was intruding upon a very important moment. A minute later, I realized the futility of my action. I still had my mask on. They couldn't see me anyway.

"I've missed you so much," she said. "Your father and I have been following the race closely. We're so proud of how far you've come."

"It's all for you. If I win the boon, I'm going to free you both."

"Oh, Orin." She pulled back. "You know we'd never ask you to put yourself in danger for us."

"You didn't," he said. "You didn't have to. How are you? Are you all right?"

She nodded slowly, and I thought I recognized the mask that fell over her features, schooling them into indifference. She didn't want Orin to know how things really were here. "We're fine. It's not ideal, but we make the best of it. At least your father and I are together. We had hoped we would run across you while you stayed here, but we feared to reach out directly. The king is very strict, and his instructions were clear. The staff was not to have any contact with the contestants."

"Why?" Orin asked.

She shook her head. "He's very paranoid. I think...It's not important. Where are you going?" She changed the subject.

"We're going..." he hesitated. "Jacq, come here. Take your mask off and meet my mother, Ramona."

I pulled my mask off hastily. "Hello, Mrs. Treebaum," I

said nervously. I couldn't believe I was meeting Orin's mother. I felt so unprepared. I hadn't dated many guys, but usually, parents liked me. This time, I wasn't so sure. What did she think about her son being with a human? Though… the camera hadn't caught our kiss, so she couldn't know we were anything other than teammates. Maybe that was for the best. No need to add potential prejudices related to interspecies dating to the list of complexities we were dealing with today.

"It's so nice to meet you, Jacqueline. Thank you so much for looking out for Orin."

"Looking out for me?" Orin scoffed. "If it wasn't for me, Jacq would run into danger any chance she got."

"You take care of each other," Ramona said. "You make a good team. It's clear to anyone who's watching that you're the strongest team."

That was nice to hear. We hadn't been able to see any of the dynamics of the other teams, other than the short time we'd been partnered with them in the Elemental Trial. And then we were all on our guard. It was crazy to think that the public, who had nothing to do with the race, knew more about parts of it than we did.

"Orin, it's dangerous for you to be out here, out of your room. The king's instructions were clear." It seemed she couldn't miss an opportunity to mother him. It was kind of sweet, really. "And why the masks? The invisibility?"

"We're going to see Jacq's sister," Orin said. He looked at me with a questioning glance, and though I appreciated it, I nodded. I didn't think Orin's mom was going to spill the beans about Cass. "We think there is something going on. With the race, and a group called the Brotherhood of the Rose and Thistle. We think Jacq's sister has something to do with it, but we're not exactly sure."

"The Brotherhood?" Ramona's dark eyes widened.

"You know of them?" I asked, eagerly.

"Oh, yes. It's not common knowledge, but if you pay attention, you see signs of their work here in the palace. The king is deeply involved in the group. There have been humans visiting here for the past few months, involved in clandestine meetings. Shipments of things that are squirreled away under the utmost secrecy."

"Faerwild and Earth used to be joined together. We think the Brotherhood is trying to merge both realms again," I offered our theory. "Do you think the king would support something like that?"

"Expanding his power over millions of more souls? Humans, who are helpless against magic and could be controlled and potentially used for his purposes? Yes, I think that's something Vale Obanstone would be extremely interested in. Your father—" She froze as the sound of heels clicking on marble reached all of our ears at the same time. "Hide!" she hissed, and Orin and I fumbled with our masks, tying them back on. Just in time, for around the corner, spun the Faerie King himself. With none other than Patricia at his side.

"Ah, Ramona. I've been looking for you. We have need of your magic."

My hand fumbled for Orin's invisible one, and I found it at his side, balled into a fist.

"Of course, Your Majesty," Orin's beautiful mother curtseyed. Anger lit inside of me at the thought of this beautiful sweet woman being enslaved to that asshole for one-hundred years.

Patricia gave a fake smile and spun on her stiletto, with Ramona following after the odd pair like a faithful hound. I felt Orin move to follow, and it was all I could do to keep hold of his hand as he moved, towed along in his wake. I couldn't do anything without risking exposing us to the king, not hold Orin back or hiss at him to stop. All I could do was follow helplessly as we slipped through a set of double doors before the king closed us all in together.

BUY NOW!

ABOUT J.A. ARMITAGE

J.A lives in a total fantasy world (because reality is boring right?) When she's not writing all the crazy fun in her head, she can be found eating cake, designing pretty pictures and hanging upside down from the tallest climbing frame in the local playground while her children look on in embarrassment. She's travelled the world working as everything from a banana picker in Australia to a Pantomime clown, has climbed to the top of Mount Kilimanjaro and the bottom of the Grand Canyon and once gave birth to a surrogate baby for a friend of hers.

She spends way too much time gossiping on Facebook and if you want to be part of her Reading Army, where you'll get lots of freebies, exclusive sneak peeks and super secret sales, join up here https://www.subscribepage.com/v7o8l

ABOUT CLAIRE LUANA

Claire Luana grew up in Seattle reading everything she could get her hands on and writing every chance she could. Eventually, adulthood won out, and she turned her writing talents to more scholarly pursuits, going to work as a commercial litigation attorney.

While continuing to practice law, Claire decided to return to her roots and try her hand once again at creative writing. She has written and published four fantasy series: the Moonburner Cycle, the Confectioner Chronicles, the Knights of Caerleon (co-written with Jesikah Sundin), and The Faerie Race (co-written with J.A. Armitage).

She lives in Seattle, Washington with her husband and two dogs. In her (little) remaining spare time, she loves to hike, travel, binge-watch CW shows, and of course, fall into a good book.

Connect with Claire Luana online at:

Website & Blog: http://www.claireluana.com
Facebook: http://www.facebook.com/claireluana
Twitter: http://www.twitter.com/clairedeluana
Goodreads: https://www.goodreads.com/author/show/15207082.Claire_Luana
Instagram: http://www.instagram.com/claireluana

ALSO BY J.A. ARMITAGE

Reverse Fairytales

Charm

Lucky Charm

Charmed

Dark Water

Blue Water

Breakwater

Dragon Slayer

Slayer

Warrior

Protector

The Faerie Race

The Sorcery Trial

The Elemental Trial

The Doomsday Trial

ALSO BY CLAIRE LUANA

Moonburner Cycle

Moonburner, Book One

Sunburner, Book Two

Starburner, Book Three

Burning Fate, Prequel Novella

Confectioner Chronicles

The Confectioner's Guild, Book One

The Confectioner's Coup, Book Two

The Confectioner's Truth, Book Three

The Confectioner's Exile, Prequel Novella

The Knights of Caerleon, with Jesikah Sundin

The Fifth Knight, Book One

The Third Curse, Book Two

The First Gwenevere, Book Three

The Faerie Race

The Sorcery Trial (Faerie Race book one)

The Elemental Trial (Faerie Race book two)

The Doomsday Trial (Faerie Race book three)

Orion's Kiss

www.ingramcontent.com/pod-product-compliance
Lightning Source LLC
Chambersburg PA
CBHW050526190726
48284CB00003B/956